Introduction

A fictional amble through a not so .typical family life.
The story revolves around the main character Mary, with several twists, turns and complications along the way.
Tony her long term discreet romance, whom she thought she'd met twenty five years ago, provides the first quirk in the story.
Mary's husband Thomas, went missing somewhere in Asia, assumed killed in 1983, but his past life continues to create serious disruptions for Mary and her family.
The story begins in 2007 with the wedding of Mary's daughter Gillian, and extends over the following decade.
If you like the unusual and the unexpected read on and I hope you enjoy.

ooooooooo

To follow on from this story please read the sequel titled "Missis Hooper" Also for sale on Amazon £4.99

Mary

CHAPTER ONE

The headlights illuminated the narrow drive access between the brick piers as Mary carefully positioned her fourteen year old silver Mercedes within a couple of feet of the garage door. Too tired to bother garaging the vehicle she collected her evening bag and quietly closed the driver's door. As she emerged from the shadow of the garage, her four bedroom detached property and surrounding area became flooded in light from the newly installed security system.

Mary quickly unlocked and entered through the front door. Once inside she kicked off her shoes and hastily went into the kitchen, switching on the lights on the way. She looked back at the partly glazed front door to see the outside return to darkness. "Thank goodness". She muttered to herself, imagining what the awakened neighbours would be thinking at this unearthly hour of the night. Although feeling worn out and exhausted from the long day and from dancing all evening, she still found the energy to practice a few rumba steps on the smooth tiled kitchen floor while waiting for her milk to warm in the microwave.

Relying on the moonlight to find her way around her bedroom she placed her mug of warm sweetened milk on the bedside table. As she sat propped up in bed she could look through the side of the bay window towards the sea front. Watching the moon glistening on the water and feeling unable to sleep, her thoughts returned to recollect that she had earlier in that day walked her daughter Gillian down the aisle to be married.

Mary took on this duty as her husband Thomas, a foreign correspondent working at the time for a daily national newspaper had been reported missing somewhere in Asia in nineteen eighty three, twenty four years ago, assumed killed.

The wedding had been perfect, her eldest son Thomas, the groom's best friend was the best man with a couple of Gillian's teacher school friends as bridesmaids.

The reception at the Oakland Hall Hotel just off the sea front for the congregation of about forty guests was followed with a dance in the evening in the hotel ballroom, with the music provided by a very smartly dressed trio consisting of two young men, one playing a keyboard, and the other the drums, accompanied by a more mature attractive lady vocalist.

The evening was attended by a further twenty or so friends and their partners. The musicians balanced the age groups perfectly by playing a fair mix of dance styles. Although Tony her long time friend was Mary's dance partner, there was several other gentlemen wishing to waltz this slim elegant good looking lady across the floor.

For the last half hour of the evening Mary had slumped into one of the chairs surrounding the floor before collecting her grey and cream checked costume jacket from the cloakroom. On returning to the ballroom to say her 'good nights'. "Now is the hour" sweetly sang the lady vocalist. Almost immediately with her jacket over one arm, Tony appeared beside her and danced Mary around the floor to the last waltz.

As the guests began to leave, Gillian Hines nee Hooper and Robert Stewart Hines the proud newly wedded couple stood in the doorway and embraced and thanked everyone in turn. Mary thought to herself. 'That was a wonderful day'.

Sunday morning arrived for Mary about half past ten as the bright warm sunlight streamed through the windows, eventually dazzling her closed eyes. Slowly she reached to lift the ornate silver framed photograph of her then forty years old handsome husband Thomas, wondering what he would look like today if he was he still alive. She carefully replaced it next to the matching framed photograph of her three children, Thomas, Daniel and Gillian as she eased her feet on to the carpeted floor.

As Mary approached the front door to collect the local 'Cornish Journal' and gather up all the loose material that had spilled from out of the newspaper on to the floor, she became aware of a figure the other side of the door. Tony grinned as the door was opened.

"You forgot I was coming round, didn't you ? I did tell you I was going to cut your hedges this morning, I guessed you weren't listening last night".

Tony took the garage key from it's hook by the kitchen door. "Would you like a coffee before you start ?" Mary asked. "If I do that I'll never start". Tony replied, smiling as he returned from the garage carrying the hedge trimmer and a rake.

After an hour or so the noise from the hedge trimmer ceased, Mary could see Tony was now clearing away the clippings. "I'll have that drink in a few minutes". Tony shouted from half way down the garden.

"Hot work today out there". Tony remarked as he sat at the kitchen table in front of a mug of coffee with beads of sweat appearing on his forehead.

"Fancy a stroll and a drink later ?" Tony asked as they walked down the drive to his car parked at the kerbside. "That would be lovely, eight o'clock as usual". Mary replied as Tony started the engine.

Mary stood on the pavement and watched as the car moved away from the kerb, a hand waving through the open window as it accelerated out of view.

Mary closed the front door behind her and retrieved a dog eared A4 students notepad from the desk in the hallway, then settled into a comfortable armchair in the corner of the lounge overlooking the rear garden. 'Hedge looks neat'. She thought to herself as she thumbed through the pages of the notepad.

Rekindling her lifelong ambition to attempt to write a fictional novel based around her family life, using her vast knowledge as an ex librarian and being extremely well educated she perused the passages and notes she had recorded to assist the plot, and among the scribbled items her attention was drawn to one particular page listing her family history.

This being a rough draft for the 'introduction' when she first started a year ago, having not as yet decided the change of the characters identities and no thoughts as to a title, Mary began to read silently to herself.

Mary Dawson was born in 1942 in a village a few miles from Warwick. She met her husband Thomas Hooper when they were both 16 years old while on holiday in Dorset with her older sister Susan. Thomas lived in Plymouth so Mary was surprised when he turned up on her doorstep a couple of weeks later. He eventually secured a job with a local newspaper in Birmingham. In 1961 after a three year courtship, at the very young age of 19 they were married in Mary's village church. By now Mary had completed her extra years at college and they made the decision to return to live in Thomas's home town where they rented a two bedroom flat. Thomas, their first child was born in 1971. By now, both having very well paid occupations, Thomas a journalist and Mary a chief librarian, they were able to take out a mortgage on a house of their own. This took them twenty miles West to a small Cornish seaside town, the four bedroom property where Mary still lives. Two years later Daniel was born and with Thomas now spending more time in foreign countries Mary was forced to give up her career to care for her two young children. She was however fortunate to have the services of a friendly neighbour to look after her children one day a week to allow her a brief social life, albeit just a visit to the local tea dance. On January 3th 1983 Mary waved goodbye to Thomas as his train departed from Plymouth station en route to London, little knowing it would be the last time she would ever see him. He'd been home for Christmas after a four month assignment in South Africa and was now being posted to Lebanon in Asia. He was last reported as leaving

Beirut on a military vehicle on 6th of February. These dates now embedded in Mary's mind. Mary's third child, Gillian was born later that year without Thomas knowing she ever existed. The previous year at the tea dance on Mary's 40th birthday she first met Anthony Pennel and the two have remained very closest of friends ever since.

Mary flicked through the pages to her last recorded note, then added further information about Gillian's wedding. She closed the scruffy looking pad.

"One day, maybe". She sighed to herself as she tossed it on to the coffee table a few feet away, Mary reached for the local newspaper which lay on the floor at her feet, and with her reading glasses still in position she settled back into the comfort of the arm chair.

Mary heard Tony insert his door key as she expected at exactly eight o'clock. "Two minutes". Mary shouted as Tony waited in the open doorway, standing tall and slim in his lightweight beige suit, his grey hair slightly thinning, but still very handsome for a man of sixty five.

The half an hour walk through the quiet lanes in the warm evening sunshine to the country pub was a regular Sunday pass time.

"Hello you two". Came a welcome from one of the locals leaning on the bar nursing a pint of bitter. "Evening Stan". Mary and Tony echoed as they wandered through to their usual table in the lounge bar.

"Dry white ?" Tony asked Mary, as if the question was really necessary. Tony went back to join Stan in the public bar to obtain his drinks. "How did the wedding go ? Was yesterday wasn't it ?" Stan enquired. "Went very well, no hitches, weather was perfect, it couldn't have gone better". Tony answered.

"Evening Tony, usual ?" Jack the elderly landlord asked. "It was a good day yesterday then". He added having overheard Tony's response to Stan.

"What's Stan on about next door ?" Mary asked as Tony returned carrying a glass of wine and his usual pint of lager. "Oh....just asking how the wedding went".

"You know I'm changing my car tomorrow, your Tom's off work so he's coming to Exeter with me". Tony said. "Are you still settled on having the car you showed me ?" "You mean the Mazda...I'm not sure. The garage say they've just had a twelve month old S Class Merc arrive in the showroom, so I'm going to have a look at that first. Mind you it's almost double the price of the Mazda". "We'll have matching vehicles then, what colour is it ? I hope it's not silver". Mary stated. "Do you know, I never asked".

After about an hour and a further drink each, Tony and Mary began the return stroll hand in hand. The evening light fading as they reached Mary's house.

"You're coming in for a coffee ?" Mary assumed as they approached the front door. "It's a bit late now Mary, I've got one or two things to sort out for tomorrow, so I'll say goodnight and see you Tuesday, pick you up at two". The couple kissed discreetly in the porch and Mary remained on the step and watched as Tony drove from sight.

CHAPTER TWO

The warm sunshine greeted Mary as she closed her front door on this pleasant Monday morning in late July. Wearing only a printed blue and cream cotton dress, she strolled the hundred yards or so from her house to the promenade and crossed the road and carefully lowered herself down the two foot drop onto the sandy beach. Putting on her dark sun glasses to shield her eyes from the glare, and with the sea gently lapping the shore, Mary set off on the smooth hard sand at the waters edge to walk the half mile journey into town.

After a leisurely fifteen minute stroll, weaving in and out of many family groups playing on the beach. Mary hopped up the wooden set of steps back on to the promenade. Balancing on one leg in turn she removed the sand from her sandals. A lull in the shore road traffic allowed Mary to safely cross to the opposite pavement and enter through the open door of the small corner shop owned by her son Daniel and his wife Debra.

The shop although minimal in size has been cleverly laid out in aisles as a mini market selling a limited range of food goods. The store also acts as a news agents while also catering for holiday visitors' beach requirements.

As Debra was busily attending to several customers Mary wandered to the rear of the store to the newspaper section. After reading the front page headlines of several daily papers she selected a couple of ladies magazines together with her usual paper. With her chosen reading material Mary queued behind the remaining two young attractive lady customers who appeared to be together. Mary assumed as they were both dressed suitably for the beach in coloured shorts, bikini tops and flip flops, and by their Welsh accents they were most certainly on holiday.

Debra was still unaware of Mary's presence as she chatted and shared a joke with the Welsh ladies. "Where in Wales have you come from ?" She asked as she handed the one lady the change. "I live in Bridgend and my sister here lives in Swansea. We came down last Saturday for a fortnight, suppose we'd better get back to our husbands and the kids before they think we've run off and left them...now there's an idea". As they left the shop laughing hilariously Debra wished them both a happy holiday and hoped the lovely weather would continue.

"Oops, Mary, never saw you there". "They sounded a jolly pair". Mary remarked still smiling at their comments. "Yes they were lovely, I wish all my customers were as pleasant.

Anyway Mary how are you after Saturday night, I don't think you ever left the dance floor, what with all the other fellas Tony looked a bit miffed". "He's alright, I can dance with him anytime. I noticed you and Daniel had a bit of style, must have been those lessons me and Tony have been giving you". "Yes, I never thought I'd ever get Daniel on to a dance floor, certainly not to do ballroom, it was great".

"Where is he ?" Mary asked. "The wholesalers dropped us short on a couple of items, so he's off chasing them up. He shouldn't be long now, he's been gone over an hour". Debra continued the conversation.

"I thought Tom made a smashing best man for Robert, especially as they both wore very smart immaculate matching suits. How long have they known each other ?".

"Oh since Robert was sixteen. They met when Robert had a trial at Tom's club, apparently he did well and he's played in the first team with Tom ever since. It was Thomas that got him his first date with our Gillian". Mary answered.

Mary stepped back from the counter as a couple with three young children approached to be served. "Gillian and Robert are off on honeymoon tomorrow then". Debra stated talking over the heads of her customers. Her sales professionalism returned as the three children, firstly the two very young girls then their elder brother all insisted on paying for their purchases themselves. Debra chatted with each of them in turn making them feel very grown up. "Thank you very much, say thank you to the lady". The mother instructed the children as they left the shop. A loud chorus of "thank you" from the pavement left Debra laughing.

"Yes, Robert's uncle and his mother are dropping them at Southampton docks on their way home. They've been staying with Gillian and Robert for the wedding".

"Me and Daniel could do with a good holiday, a Caribbean cruise would be lovely, I wish. We managed a week in Torquay for our honeymoon, and that was in a caravan".

"Yes, I remember. We did a little better, me and Thomas had a week in Dorset in a holiday flat, and that was self catering. Anyway enough of our woes, you've got a queue forming, I'll be off before I start loosing you your customers. See you soon".

Mary left the cool of the shop as she sidestepped around a young mum and her two children busily choosing from the array of beach items from the many containers situated at the back of the pavement set against the shop front. Mary continued her walk in the hot midday sunshine and reached the small town centre within a few minutes.

After a modest purchase of a light lunch and a smart fashionable sun hat from the indoor shopping mall, now refreshed, and with the hat sitting stylishly on her head she crossed back to the sea front for the return stroll home along the promenade.

In the cool of her lounge with the sun now having moved round to the west, Mary relaxed with a cup of tea and her thoughts returned to the wedding and how Gillian and Robert first met.

Robert worked at the nearby caravan park at the time and arrived one Saturday lunchtime with Mary's eldest son Thomas on the way to play football. Gillian and Robert just smiled at each other on meeting.

The handsome sixteen year old lad must have liked her, as that same evening after the match, Thomas telephoned her at Robert's request.

They met later that night outside the local cinema and have been together ever since.

When the holiday season ended Robert and a friend from the camp rented a flat locally. Robert then enrolled at teacher training college for a couple of years and eventually secured a position at the local boys senior school.

In addition to teaching classroom subjects,

due to his sporting ability, when asked he chose to become head of sport.

Robert and his mother endured a hostile environment with his father during most of his childhood. As soon as he left school he came to work and live in Cornwall. Shortly afterwards without any warning his father walked out of the family home and to his mother's relief never returned or made contact again.

Lightening entering the bedroom through the open curtains in the early hours of the morning failed to awaken Mary. With the distant rumbling of thunder gradually growing closer, and with the strong wind driving the rain hard against the windows, it would appear that the current short heatwave had come to an end. Eventually a loud crack of thunder startled Mary from her sleep.

The next flash of lightening lit up the photographs on the bedside table. She now felt quite vulnerable all alone in the house she once shared with her husband and their children. Mary approached the side bay window, and in the light created by each flash of lightening she watched the surf spewing onto the promenade.

Returning to sit on the edge of the bed, she stared at the framed photograph of Thomas, remembering the last day he was seen and what horror he may have endured. Unable to prevent the tears running down her cheeks and with the dawn light brightening the room, she lifted herself into bed and turned away from the picture in the hope of another couple of hours sleep.

****

CHAPTER THREE

Mary stared through the lounge window watching Tony leaning on his new Mercedes, smartly dressed as ever, wearing a pale grey suit with matching open necked shirt.

"I see you bought the Merc then". Mary said as she reached her garden wall. "What do you think ?" Tony asked. "Looks very nice, you had to go one better than me, it'll make mine look tatty". Mary joked as she wandered around the vehicle inspecting the shiny pale blue bodywork.

"It's got a few miles on the clock for a year old car, eighteen thousand. Suppose that's the reason for the price". Tony added. "And how much did it cost ?" "Thirty". "Thirty thousand, goodness me". Mary gulped. "Well fifty quid short". Tony added. "Oh..that makes all the difference". Mary quipped.

"Anyway lets get going". Mary fastened her seat belt as Tony drove the car the short distance to the sea front and eastward along the promenade. "Before I forget, your Tom gave me a photo he took at the wedding, he thought you might like to take it when you visit his gran at the weekend, it's on the back seat".

After a fifteen minute trip the Mercedes entered the large hotel car park. Tony slowly passed all the vacant spaces to leave the vehicle parked in the furthermost available space possible.

"Tony, just what I need is a good walk through puddles in these new dance shoes. You'll have to hang on a bit while I change back to my shoes" "I don't know why you ever walk outside in you dance shoes". Tony remarked.

"Well it's still a damn long walk to the hotel in the wet". Mary replied annoyingly. The couple entered the hotel reception and on in to the modest size function room used for the afternoon tea dance.

The sound of 'Moon River' was being played on the keyboard with several couples gliding around the floor to the first waltz.

"You're not usually late". Les the keyboard player noted as he tinkled off the last few bars. "Very unusual". Mary answered. "He's just got a new car so we had to spend ten minutes admiring it". Mary added sarcastically. "What you bought then Tone ?" "Merc three fifty S class, it's only a year old, so it'll see me out". "Very nice". Les replied as he handed Tony his change.

Tony and Mary reached their customary table at the far side of the floor. "Take your partners for a quickstep". Les announced as the music began.

"They're off to the Caribbean today". Mary reminded Tony as they stepped onto the ballroom floor joining the other couples and saying "hello" to all the regulars seated around the edge of the floor as they danced by.

A friendly voice came from behind just as the music ended. "How was the wedding Mary ?" "Oh, hello Pat". A surprised Mary replied. "You better now, not seen you two for a few weeks ?" "Yes, I started it off with just a cold and then Philip caught it, we're both fit again".

"The wedding was perfect, everything was great, even the weather. They're off on their honeymoon today, four weeks Caribbean cruise". Mary replied to Pat's earlier question. "These youngsters know what they like, sounds lovely.

I've not seen your Gillian since I packed in my lunchtime job at her school, remember me to her next time you see her". Pat requested as the music resumed with the two couples still chatting on the ballroom floor.

"We'd better start dancing or leave the floor". Pat's husband chipped in with a laugh.

"A few strange faces in today Les". Tony commented as Les arrived at their table on his normal interval stroll to greet everyone. "Yes Tone it's probably down to the weather, those three couples are on holiday, they're staying in the hotel ". Les said as he discreetly pointed to a table in the far corner of the room. "Better wander on".

After a complete circuit of the floor Les stood by the small raised platform, one hand resting on the edge of the keyboard while drinking from a cup with the other. "Ready to go again folks ?" He called out as he began playing the next dance.

"On your own today Ted ?" Tony remarked as several couples were leaving. "Yes". The lively eighty six year old replied. "Kate's got her daughter here on holiday but she'll be back next week. Given me chance to spread myself around a bit". "Lucky girls". Mary added with a loud laugh.

After two or three brief stops on the way out of the car park to chat and have the Mercedes looked over, Tony began the return journey.

"Don't forget your photo". Tony reminded Mary as she closed the front passenger door. "It's under the newspaper". Tony added. "That's lovely, he's even put it in a frame". Mary announced as she stretched across the rear seat. "Gillian looks absolutely beautiful, just like her mother". Tony flattered.

Tony took one more admiring look around his car before smartly striding up the path to join Mary in the kitchen. "Dinner will be about an hour". Mary stated.

"I'll make a cup of tea to be going on with". "What time do you intend starting on Saturday ?" Tony asked, referring to Mary's visit to see her mother. "Hopefully be gone by seven". Mary replied.

"You know I would love to have taken you, any other weekend would have been fine". Tony said apologetically. "Don't worry about it, I know you would, it's about time I did something for myself and not keep relying on you".

"What would you say to a few days at the cottage the week after ?" Tony asked. "i think that would be lovely, we could make it a long weekend.

You do know I won't be back until late on Monday ?, I'm spending a bit of time with our Susan". Mary replied.

****

CHAPTER FOUR

The wiper blades suddenly doubled in speed as they furiously flashed from side to side across the windscreen. The satnav informed Mary of her imminent exit from the motorway. "Prepare to keep left in one quarter of a mile". The voice instructed.

With visibility severely impaired by the torrential rain and being hemmed in the central carriageway with surface spray hitting the Mercedes from the speeding vehicles from both sides, Mary now became nervous and anxious, and with her near side indicator apparently being ignored, she was almost ready to abort the manoeuvre.

Finally at the last possible moment and to her great relief a friendly lorry flashed it's headlights a couple of times allowing Mary to change lanes just in time to leave the motorway. "Now turn left". The voice said interrupting Mary's concentration. "Bit late to tell me now". Mary muttered as she allowed herself to relax having negotiated her way off the busy M5 and on to the relative calmness of the A38.

The windscreen wipers returned to a more gentle speed as the rain abated. "In three hundred yards you will have reached your destination". The satnav announced. Mary turned left between the solid looking stone piers into the car park, halting her Mercedes between the diagonal white lines against the front of the imposing new red brick building.

She stood and stretched for a few moments in the light rainy drizzle before reaching for a shopping bag from the rear seat. Proceeding up the gradual paved ramp Mary entered into the reception area. "Good morning". Came a soft voice from the smart lady seated at an expensive looking light coloured oak desk. "Are you here to visit someone ?" "To see my mother, Gillian Dawson". Mary answered. With a quick glance at a screen the attractive receptionist said "Gillian, yes she's in room seventeen.

I'm sorry but I have to ask, do you have some identification ?". "I completely understand" Mary said and produced a driving licence from her coat pocket.

"My goodness, have you just drove here this morning ?" She asked noticing the address on the licence. "Yes, but I won't try it again, I'll come on the coach or the train next time" "You must be worn out, what with this weather. I'll call Janice". She replied as she pressed a button on the desk.

A slim pretty young girl in her late teens entered through a connecting door, conspicuous by her purple hair. "This is Janice, don't be frightened by the colour, she's only purple at the weekends". The receptionist ribbed. Janice laughed and introduced herself. "Misses Hooper is here to see her mother, Gillian".

Janice took hold of Mary's hand and returned through the connecting door and into the main corridor. "Gillian's room is down at the end, number seventeen". Janice said still holding on to Mary's hand. "This is our dining room, lunch is at twelve". Janice informed as they approached an open door. Several elderly residents, mainly ladies were sat eating at tables

Through an open door on the other side of the corridor Mary could see an elderly lady eating from a lap tray accompanied by relatives with two teenage boys "This is the main lounge". Janice advised. "Some of our residents prefer to have their lunch in here, especially when they have visitors".

"Everything seems to be decorated lovely". Mary observed. "It's all brand new, the home was only opened last year, Gillian was one of our first guests, you'll find she's got a lovely room, here we are. Margaret's probably giving your mum her lunch at the moment". She quietly tapped on the door before entering. "Margaret, this is Misses Hooper, Gillian's daughter" "Mary". Mary interjected. "I'll leave you in Margaret's company". Janice said, finally releasing Mary's hand with a slight squeeze. "She's a lovely young girl". "Yes she is". Replied Margaret. "She and I are your mum's main carers".

Margaret a more mature lady, possibly in her mid forties, of sturdy appearance with blond hair and an attractive friendly face, together with Janice as Gillian's carers gave Mary the assurance she hoped for.

Mary crossed the generously sized room to her mother sitting in a chair beside the bed and gave her a kiss and a hug. There was no sign that Gillian new who Mary was. "She's finished her lunch now, Gillian..would you like to get back into bed ?". Margaret asked sympathetically. Margaret carefully assisted Gillian as she shuffled herself onto the edge of the bed, placing a couple of pillows against the headboard she lifted Gillian's legs on to the bed.

With Gillian safely and carefully propped up in bed Margaret collected the used crockery on to a tray.

"Your mum sleeps most of the time, so don't worry, she's fine otherwise". "Yes I know, my sister Susan keeps me up to date, she phones me once a week. This is my first time here, I'm too far away to come very often". Mary replied.

"We all know Susan, she livens the place up every weekend. How far have you come then ?" "That sounds like my sister. I live down in Cornwall. My husband, he died in nineteen eighty three, he came from Plymouth, so when we married in sixty one we moved down there". "No thought of moving back ?" "I couldn't do that, all my family have been brought up there. I tried to tempt our Susan but she preferred to stay where she was".

"When did you come up ?" "Just got here about half an hour ago". "You haven't driven here ?" "Yes, I started about seven this morning". "In all that rain, good God you must be exhausted. Would you like a cup of tea ? Of course you would, I'll fetch you one".

Within five minutes Margaret returned bearing a tray and placed it besides Mary, now seated in Gillian's armchair. "That's so kind". Mary thanked.

"Are you going to call on your sister ?" Margaret asked. "I'll be staying with her over the weekend, I'll be back with Susan tomorrow". "I'll leave you alone with your mum now, I'll probably see you again before you go, I'm on till two today".

Gillian stared vacantly toward the far wall, Mary spoke in a soft voice but received no recognition. Slowly Gillian closed her eyes and fell asleep. Mary rose from her chair to collect her shopping bag from by the door and removed a plastic Marks and Spencer carrier bag containing a couple of sets of new underclothes and placed them in one of the drawers in Gillian's bedside cabinet. Settling back into the armchair Mary scanned through a couple of magazines she'd purchased from Debra earlier in the week. A gentle tap on the door and Margaret re-entered. “Mum's still asleep so I was just about to go on. I've put her some new underclothes in the drawer and that photograph of her granddaughter's wedding on the table”.

“They look a happy couple, when did they get married ?” “Only last Saturday, they've just gone on a cruise for four weeks...to the Caribbean. These youngsters get their priorities right these days”. Mary added jokingly. She then leaned across the bed and gave her mum a gentle hug as she slept.

Margaret held the door open and together they strolled down the long corridor. “What are the names of your daughter and her young man ?” Margaret asked. “Gillian, after her grandma and Robert. They're both school teachers, she teaches the tiny ones and Robert's a sports master at the local senior school”.

Mary thanked Margaret and the two shook hands. “I'm not in tomorrow so have a nice weekend and a safe journey home. I look forward to seeing you again”. Margaret said as she left Mary at the door.

Mary quickly typed Susan's address into the satnav and set off as instructed in the direction of Edgbaston.

After twenty minutes the Mercedes was guided on to the nineteen sixties housing estate . Mary slowed the car to a halt outside of number three. Standing on the pavement for a while she remembered how all the houses were identical on both sides of the street. All pairs of semi-detached three bedroom two storey properties, buff coloured brickwork with painted horizontal slatting beneath the ground floor window. The only exception being the addition of a porch to a couple of the properties.

"Didn't expect you this early". Susan said as the sisters greeted each other with a hug before going inside. "Get yourself sat down and I'll make us some lunch".

"All the houses still look alike, I suppose you still have to make a note of your number before you go out anywhere ?" Mary joked. "Bit stale now that old joke". Susan replied in retaliation to what she considered a bit of a snobby remark as she tried to pass it off with a laugh.

"I thought it was funny the first time I heard it". "That was because it was me who told it". Susan quipped in her Birmingham accent.

"What was your journey like ?" "Absolutely horrendous, tipped down all the way, the motorway was like being in a speed boat race. I'll come by coach next time, I won't drive again, it was a bit frightening at times". Mary replied annoyingly.

"How did you find mum ? Did you like the new place ?" Susan asked. "Just as you've been telling me, she didn't know me and after about twenty minutes she went to sleep, I sat by her bed for an hour. The home is beautiful, it's a big improvement to the Warwick place. It must be a lot easier on you being that much closer".

"She's nearly always asleep or out of it when me and Walter visit. Very occasionally she'll have a better day and say a few words, although they don't normally make much sense. Did you meet Margaret and Janice ? They're mum's two carers". "Yes they were lovely to me and very kind to mum". "Only thing about the new place, it's very expensive, there's not going to be a lot left from the sale of mum's house, the nursing home will just about eat it all up". "I don't doubt it Susan, if it starts getting tight let me know. If there does happen to be anything left it's yours, you and Walter have had all the responsibility, I'm too far away to be involved". "We should be okay for a couple of years at least".

"Anyway, where's Walley". Mary asked with a daft grin. "Don't let him hear you say that, he gets enough off his mates, especially when he wears his Villa bobble hat. He's at the Villa now, gone to watch his beloved team. He said something about a pre-season friendly, whatever that is. He thinks more about the Villa than me", Susan replied with a good dose of sarcasm. "Never, he's not daft, he worships you". "Suppose he does, I was only joking".

"The wedding went well". Susan stated. "Yes everything was perfect, they must be half way to the Caribbean by now". Mary answered. "You will tell Gillian I want a couple of photos ?, I'll see her in a few weeks time when I come down.". "Any idea when ?". Mary asked. "I think it'll have to be after the schools restart, early in September. I just need to check with National Coaches, I'm pretty sure they go to Plymouth. Walter won't be coming, he finally found himself a job last week, so he won't want to have any time off just yet. It's only at the local garden centre, but it finds him something to do, and it keeps him in pocket money. He seems happy enough with it".

"You know you should have stayed with me for the wedding ? I did keep asking you". Mary urged. "Course I know we could have, but Walter wanted to take the chance to tour Cornwall seeing as we were already down there, that's why he hired that camper van. Mind you the village vicar didn't seem too pleased next morning when he saw us leaving his car park". "Well let me know as soon as you find out and I'll meet you at the bus station". Mary added.

"The fella you introduced me to...you seemed very fond of each other, is it serious ?" Susan asked cheekily. "That was Tony, I've known him a long time now. He's my tea dance partner...I saw you having a dance with him. We do see a lot of each other, so who knows, one day maybe.

I remember when I first met him, it was on my fortieth birthday, sixteenth of January in nineteen eighty two. Thomas and Tony never met each other but Thomas didn't worry about Tony being my dance partner. Mind you, he didn't seem to care what I was doing at that time, goodness knows what was the matter with him". Mary said sorrowfully. "He actually gave me a couple of dances at the wedding". Susan interrupted. "He seems a lovely bloke, you're a lucky girl our Mary".

"Do you remember when we first met Thomas ?" Susan asked. "I couldn't forget, we was on holiday. It was the first time we'd been allowed to go without mum and dad, do you remember that train ride to Swanage on the south coast. It took nearly all day to get there. We met him and his mate the first evening on the pier, they had followed us all along the prom before they chatted us up". Mary replied.

"Do you remember they were on a biking holiday and staying at the youth hostel and they couldn't remember which hill the hostel was on. We sat on a bench and laughed our heads off each time they came back down" Mary added..

"I seem to think that Thomas and his mate both fancied you, I can't even remember his mates name, we did get on okay after the first night though, he was alright". Susan added. "They only stayed for three days, never ever dreamt I'd see him again, then he turned up on our doorstep a few weeks later". Mary chirped. "Yes I know, I answered the door to him. I didn't know who he was until he told me". Susan replied.

"It all turned out great until we'd been married about twenty years, then I don't know what went wrong, but after Daniel was born Thomas didn't seem the same bloke. He was rarely home, and even when he was he never took any interest in me or the children. All he talked about was his next overseas assignment, and he could never get away quick enough, and he'd be gone for a couple of months at time". Mary said in despair.

"Is fish and chips alright tonight Mary ?, we've been chatting all afternoon, I never though about preparing anything for dinner. Sounds like Walter's back.....just heard the back door slam".

"Hiya Mary, good trip ?" Walter asked greeting Mary with a kiss on the cheek. "I wouldn't say that, it was terrible, too many nut cases on the motorway, you couldn't see a thing for the rain, yet nearly everybody still drove at stupid speeds".

"Mary's kept me talking all afternoon so you haven't got any dinner". Susan joked as she added. "Nip to the chip shop Walter". "Blimey Sue, I've only just walked in. What do you want ?" "He doesn't mind, the chip shop's only round the corner". Susan said as Walter grabbed his jacket from the hall rack on his way out.

Mary parked her car in the same space as the previous day. "Morning Susan, morning Misses Hooper". The lady receptionist greeted. Susan lead the way through the internal door and along the corridor, and with two gentle taps on the door entered Gillian's room. Gillian was alone and again propped up in bed with a couple of pillows. The sisters sat in the chairs either side of the bed and held Gillian's hands as they rested on top of the covers.

"I think she's aware of us this morning, she seems more alert than usual. Mum it's Susan and Mary". Susan said hopefully expecting a flicker of recognition.

Mary placed Gillian and Robert's wedding photograph on the bed for their mum to see. The sisters gave each other a knowing glance as they observed a tear appear in the corners of Gillian's eyes. "You remember your lovely granddaughter". Mary said in a soft voice. " She's all grown up now, a beautiful young woman". Mary continued.

"Susan". Mary whispered across the bed. "How come we just marched straight in ? I had to sign in and show some identification yesterday, and then Janice held my hand all the way to mum's room". "Once they know you they don't worry, Janice is very touchy feely anyway, but she is a sweet kid and treats mum like her own". Susan replied. Susan, the elder of the sisters by just one year looked very young wearing a cream and lime green striped sweater and navy blue pleated skirt. Mary attributed her youthful look to never having the worries of bringing up children.

Susan wandered over to, and collected a framed photograph from a cabinet on the far side of the room. "Did you see this old photo ?" She asked Mary. "I found this when we cleared out mum's house. I thought it was a nice picture of mum and dad so I had it enlarged, I thought it might help bring back some memories for her". By now Gillian had drifted off to sleep.

"We might as well make a move and see what Walter's up to". Both sisters leaned over the bed and gave Gillian a kiss before making their way back to the reception area. Janice appeared via a side door carrying a tray of used cups and saucers. “Hello you two, almost missed you. How did you find your mum ? I thought she seemed quite bright this morning”. Janice chirped in her high pitched friendly voice. “Yes we thought that, I'm sure she knew we were there”. Susan replied. “We're going now, so I'll see you next time”. Susan added as she pulled open the main door to be greeted by the mid-day sunshine. “I hope it's like this for my journey tomorrow”. Mary stated as the Mercedes left the car park.

Although the sun wasn't shining the forecast was for a dry day. Susan and Walter leaned on the Mercedes wishing Mary a safe journey. “Ring me the minute you get home”. Susan instructed. “I'll let you know in a couple of days when I can come down”. She added. “It's all right for some, I've got to work”. Walter quipped at the same time with his head through Mary's open window to give her a kiss.

“You couldn't stand retirement then”. Mary said. “I had to have something, I was beginning to drive Susan mad. It's not much of a job, general dogs body, tidying and watering plants. Still it gets me out.

Anyway, it's a long trip on your own, so drive safely and hope to see you soon”. “Yes be careful” Susan added. Susan and Walter stood on the pavement and waved as the Mercedes took the first turning on the left and out of sight.

Forty minutes later Mary was back on the motorway heading south along the thick blue line of the satnav.

With the M5 now several miles behind her, Mary headed for Plymouth and across the Tamar bridge to familiar territory. Turning the silver Mercedes off the sea front and drawing to a halt on the driveway with a crunching of shingle beneath the tyres, Mary gave a sigh of relief to be back home.

Picking up the post and the junk mail that had landed on the hall mat over the weekend she stepped into the kitchen. A few moments later she launched herself full length onto the settee in the lounge with a hot mug of coffee.

During the following couple of hours the telephone rang numerous times, the answering machine also played it's part in trying to awaken her. Finally the constant ringing tone eventually brought Mary out of her deep sleep.

Taking the almost full mug of cold coffee to the sink she wearily picked up the telephone receiver from the hall table. “Mary, it's Susan”. Came the anxious voice. “Are you alright ?” “Yes, I'm fine, sorry Susan I've been asleep ever since I got in”. “Just needed to know you'd got back safely. I've rung three or four times”. “I can see that by the answer machine”. “Sorry to wake you up, but I'm happier now I've spoken to you. I'll ring you again next week., Bye Mary”.

With the conversation concluded Mary slid into her slippers and went out to her car, scuffing in the loose chippings of the recently laid driveway. She lifted a holdall from the car boot and feeling the coolness of the August evening air on her bare arms, she hurriedly returned to the warmth of the house, pointing the key fob in the direction of the Mercedes as she entered through the front door.

****

CHAPTER FIVE

"I had a phone call from Gillian late last night" Mary informed Tony as they skipped around the floor to the tempo of the quickstep. "She says to thank you for the wonderful surprise wedding present. You never told me you'd upgraded their cabin".

The music ended and they crossed the floor back to their table. "You made a mess of that dance". Mary mocked. "I can't hear the timing and listen to your chatter at the same time". Tony replied. "I didn't tell you because I know you, it wouldn't have been a secret for long, you wouldn't have been able to resist telling Gillian". Mary jumped in sharply "While we're on the subject of secrets, Gillian made me promise not to let you know she'd told me, so don't go saying anything.

She told me you gave her the money for the deposit on their cottage a couple of years ago. Why didn't you tell me ?" "I thought you might think I was interfering too much if you'd known about it". "No, I think it was lovely and very generous of you. I know you think the world of Gillian",. Mary said admiringly. "I always intended to help her, they had no chance of saving enough to get a mortgage". Tony added.

"What did Gillian have to say about the cruise ?" "She said they'd been to Madeira and they now had a few days at sea. But she was really excited with the cabin. She said it was one of the superior cabins on the top deck with their own balcony. She said she'll give you a big kiss when they get home".

"That sounds like the cheeky monkey". Tony joked.

"We'd better have a dance or Les will think we don't like his music". Tony commented as they stepped onto the ballroom floor and glided smoothly with the flow as Les sang 'Magic Moments', doing a respectable impersonation of Perry Como to the tempo of the foxtrot..

Mary has cooked an evening meal for her and Tony now almost every night for as long as she can remember, especially after the Tuesday tea dance.

So it was a bit of a surprise to Tony when she suggested that she wanted to thank him for his generosity to Gillian. “Don't go changing into your grunge, I'm treating you to a meal out tonight, I've booked dinner at 'The Italians' restaurant for eight o'clock”. “When did you do that ?” Tony asked in bewilderment. “When you went to the toilets at the dance, to thank you”. “What for ?” “For Gillian, what you've done for her”. “Well we both know why I would do something to help her”

To change the conversation Tony began discussing her weekend trip. “My sister Susan is going to come down for a week or two sometime next month”. Mary advised. “I had a couple of dances with her at the wedding”. Tony replied. “She can't half dance”.

“Yes she is good, our mum and dad lived for dancing and they taught us both from when we were kids. Susan took it more seriously than me and she went to professional ballroom and Latin lessons for a couple of years. Unfortunately she married Walter, and he's got two left feet. No....I didn't mean that to sound like that, Walter's a smashing bloke, dancing is not his thing”. Mary paused reflecting on what she'd just said.

“Mind you I can't say a lot, my husband would never take me dancing, or anywhere else for that matter, especially after Daniel was born. He never bothered about me going out with friends or going dancing with you”. “He sounds a funny bloke, must have been very trusting”. Tony remarked. “Thomas was always away working abroad.

At that time, with little ones on my own I had to give up my career. If it hadn't been for my neighbour Jan, from next door looking after the children for me one day a week, I'd never have gone out. I wouldn't have met you". "I can thank Jan for bringing us together then ?" Tony chirped.

"The best thing I ever did was to go and learn to dance, I wouldn't have met you at that tea dance on your birthday if I hadn't". Tony added. "You were my birthday present". Mary said with sincerity.

"Mind you I remember being kicked around the floor a bit that afternoon". Mary joked. "Well I was a bit nervous and still guessing most of the steps". "Anyway you've turned out okay, lets get ready and go out for a nice meal". Mary said.

****

CHAPTER SIX

Mary shivered as she stood waiting in the open doorway gazing towards the sea front. The B & B signs on several of the private properties swinging in the strong cool breeze on this early Friday morning.

The thought of opening her four bedroom house for holiday guests was something Mary had never considered. She watched as the pale blue Mercedes turned off the promenade and a smiling Tony pulled up across the drive entrance.

"I don't know what you're grinning at, I've been standing here for ten minutes in the cold". Mary called out angrily. "Why didn't you stay inside ?" "I'm ready waiting, you're never late, I just kept thinking you'll be here any minute". Mary snapped back.

The pair crossed paths as Tony went to collect Mary's bags from the porch step. Tony placed the bags on the rear seats and climbed into the car beside Mary.

"Sorry I'm a bit late, I didn't realise the time". "You're not that late it's just that it's a bit chilly this morning". Mary said apologetically. "I slammed your front door, I hope you've got your key". "Yes, lets go". Mary urged.

The Mercedes moved off along Mary's street heading for the A38 then westward towards the tip of Cornwall.

Tony a born and bred Cornish man pointed to his town of birth as the sign for Redruth appeared. "Yes I know, you've told me so many times". Mary said sarcastically.

Anthony Pennel was an only child, his parents moved from Redruth to be nearer to his father's workplace in Plymouth when he was just two years old. After his parents died, first his mother eight years ago, followed by his father four years later in

2003. Tony inherited both the family home and a holiday cottage at Sennen near to Lands End..

Tony reversed the car across the grass verge into the parking space reserved for Blackthorn Cottage. Mary crossed the lane from the small parking area and unlocked the front door of the cottage while Tony followed with the weekend bags.

Blackthorn being the extreme right hand cottage in a row of three pairs of pretty semi-detached single storey dwellings. The other five properties all owned by a local resident and used exclusively as holiday lets.

Although Blackthorn is privately owned by Tony, he still has a responsibility to pay a nominal yearly maintenance fee for outside areas and the upkeep of the private lane.

All six homes identically decorated with white rendered walls with pale grey doors and window frames, and stone roofs. A short paved path leads from the the grass verge to the front door with a small neatly tendered lawn to the side.

"I've brought some eggs, bacon, and beans, what would you like for lunch ? Oh, and some cheese if you fancy a sandwich". Mary asked. "Beans on toast would be great, two rounds". Tony replied.

After a leisurely lunch they strolled arm in arm down the steep hill to Sennen beach in the pleasant warm afternoon sunshine. The return walk being a more daunting task, The weather had again become more distinctively cool and combined with the effort needed to ascend Cove Hill, the sight of the cottage was a great relief. Once inside Tony immediately switched on both bars of the electric fire.

The next morning a layer of mist drifted across the lane as the sun warmed the damp surface after the overnight rainfall.

"I think we'll drive down this morning". Tony said, while standing looking out from the living room window at the Mercedes parked on the opposite side of the lane. "We didn't have a lot of time yesterday, and I wouldn't want to face that walk again". Mary added.

The Mercedes reached the bottom of the hill and proceeded along the sea front, negotiating the narrow bends before entering the car park. "The car park's looking a bit full". Tony proclaimed. "Well it is a Saturday, and the holiday season, you can't expect anything else". Mary muttered. Fortunately a vehicle began to vacate a position as Tony approached, and just as fortunate the preceding car also searching for a space hadn't noticed the departing driver's intentions. Tony pulled the Mercedes at an angle to assert his determination to occupy the parking bay, and carefully reversed into the narrow space. "No ones going to scratch it....I saw you checking the cars each side of you. They both look brand new". Mary ribbed as Tony rejoined her as she waited near the pay machine after attaching his ticket to the inside of his windscreen.

"What do you suggest ?" Tony asked. "Let's just wander about, we can have a wander in the lifeboat station and the Roundhouse. Then we can walk to the other end of the prom".

"I fancy some fish and chips for lunch a bit later". Tony said as they were attracted to a group of people leaning on the sea wall. Tony and Mary tagged on the end of the row of onlookers. "What's the fascination ? It's the boat". Tony said pointing a short distance out to sea. "It's being followed by a group of dolphins, there must be a couple of dozen of them". The line of men, women and children, family by family gradually vacated the sea wall. as the dolphin display ended.

Two hours later after their stroll and promised lunch, and with the sun now feeling quite hot, Tony and Mary returned to the car park. “Don't panic, no ones scratched this side”. Mary chirped as she carefully opened the door and squeezed through the tight gap into the passenger seat.

With the car safely installed back in the cottage parking space and the afternoon very hot, Tony and Mary spent the rest of the day lounging in the tiny rear garden in the shade of a neighbouring tree.

“I'll have a wander to the shop for a Sunday paper while you're cooking breakfast”. Tony informed. “Bring me something nice”. Mary joked, knowing the limitations of the shop.

“Where to today ?” Tony asked as he wiped the last of the egg yoke from his plate with a slice of bread. “I'm not walking all day, somewhere in the car”. “Yes but where would you like to go ?” Tony asked again. “I don't know, somewhere”. Mary sighed hopelessly. “Let's see where we get to”. Tony replied.

“We're almost back on the A thirty”. Tony said after cruising along the lonely narrow lanes. “Which way. Left or right ?” He urged. “Too late to choose now....oh well, we're going left”.

Within a short distance the sign for St. Ives appeared on the roadside. “Next left”. Mary ordered. “Saint Ives, let's go there, we went there the last time we came to the cottage”. “Maybe not such a good idea”. Tony said as he left the A30 and no sooner joined the tail end of a line of stationery vehicles on the A3047.

“This queue probably goes all the way to Saint Ives”. “How much further is it ?” Mary asked as Tony inched the car forward a few yards. “It's only a couple of miles, but it's going to be packed.

What do you reckon, shall we keep going or try somewhere else ?" Tony asked. By now several cars were taking it in turns to reverse into a disused farm entrance and cross over to the almost empty carriageway and leave in the opposite direction. This created a brief surge forward for the frustrated vehicle occupants.

'Welcome to St. Ives' invited the sign as they eventually reached their destination. "Well we've got here". Tony said with a sigh of relief. "Now the hard bit, finding somewhere to park". "Is there a park and ride ?" Mary enquired. "Must be one somewhere...... God knows where. Here's a car park". Tony replied, and followed a couple of other cars hopelessly looking for a vacant space. Luckily on arriving at the far side of the car park an attendant was just opening the gates to allow access into an adjacent field as an overflow facility. Tony followed the previous vehicles and gratefully accepted the space as directed by the steward. "That was a stroke of luck". Tony commented as the steady flow of eager motorists gradually filtered in and covered the green field.

"Have you noticed, car parks around here are always at the top of a steep hill ?" Mary moaned. "Sod it". She cursed, stubbing her toe on a raised paving as they descended toward the harbour.

"I'm starving, let's find somewhere to have lunch before we start wandering". Tony said. "What about this place ?" Mary suggested, pointing to the menu board displayed on the wall adjacent to the entrance. "I think we've been in here before, looks pretty busy, let's see if there's a table"

After strolling around the harbour and the narrow back lanes, including traipsing in and out of many of the local artist studios, eventually resulting in the unnecessary purchase of a water colour print, the couple made their way wearily up the steep hill back to the car park. Tony uncomfortably changing the wrapped framed 18 inch by 36 inch picture from under one arm and then the other. "This is an awkward thing to carry, for sixty quid you'd expect to get a handle" Tony joked breathlessly. "Stop making a fuss, we're here now". Mary quipped while laughing quietly following a few steps behind.

"It looks like changeover day, there's three different cars in now". Mary observed as Tony returned the Mercedes to it's reserved cottage parking space.

True to forecast, Mary opened the bedroom curtains to be greeted by heavy rain bouncing off the tarmac in the lane creating small fast flowing rivers against the grass verges.

"They were right, the weather girl said we were going to have rain for most of the day. I don't think it's worth hanging around twiddling our thumbs all day, we might as well pack up and go on home". Tony suggested".

"You tidy the bedroom and I'll sort the kitchen". Mary replied.

Tony rushed back and forth across the lane loading the Mercedes, with water dripping from his head and sodden jacket. Back in the cottage he grabbed a towel from the bathroom and rubbed furiously at his head and shoulders, removed his jacket and threw it into a plastic bag together with the wet towel. "Is it still raining ?" Mary joked while unable to prevent a bout of giggling. "You need laugh, you'll find out for yourself in a minute". Tony added referring to Mary standing undercover in the cottage doorway. Tony slammed the cottage door shut and they both made a dash for the Mercedes. "Damn it". Tony cursed. "It's locked itself". He cursed again as he fumbled in his trouser pocket for the key. By now Mary stood cowering under an umbrella she belatedly decided to open.

Finally all steamed up and sat in the dryness of the car Tony started the engine and with the wiper blades swishing across the windscreen the Mercedes moved out of the cottage parking space and on through the narrow lanes back towards the A30.

Silence descended inside the car, the only noise being the smooth purr of the engine and the soft roaring made by the tyres on the wet road surface.

Tony's intention on this last day of their weekend break was to once again ask to marry Mary. The silence continued as Tony glanced at Mary, at sixty five years old, still a strikingly attractive woman, even with her soaking wet hair crimped and frizzed. Eventually the long period of quiet was ended.

"Don't say it". Mary ordered as a road sign for Redruth came in to view. "As if I would". Tony joked. "But I would like to ask if you've thought any more about us getting married ?" Tony nervously asked. Mary tried to ignore the question and began to look at herself in the visor mirror while forcing a comb through her drying hair. "Well ?" Tony urged. "I can't stop thinking that Thomas is still alive, I know it's silly but he could be living another life somewhere. I could never understand him, we had a fantastic life from the day we met until shortly after Daniel was born, then it all seemed to change. He started taking on more and more, and longer overseas assignments, I hardly ever saw him. I can't help hoping that he didn't come to any harm and he is still alive somewhere".

"After all he was a war correspondent working in some of the most dangerous places. All the investigators came to the conclusion that he must have been murdered or had some sort of fatal accident. I know I never met him but it sounds as if you still have some feeling for him". Tony paused for thought. "You still have his photo by your bed although you've got one of me there as well". "I've only left that there for the sake of the children, after all he is their father and I wouldn't want them to think that I'd forgotten all about him". Mary answered. "So can we just stay as we are, we've been together now for twenty five years so we can wait a bit longer, can't we ?" "I suppose so, but I will keep asking". Tony replied.

After a further spell of silence and with no significant change in the weather the Mercedes finally came to a halt at the kerbside outside of Mary's house.

In an instant Tony hovered over Mary with an open umbrella as she stepped out of the car. Mary looked down at her shoes submerged in a couple of inches of trapped water. "I appreciate the brolly but you could have got a bit closer to the kerb". Mary cursed, wading to the footpath. Mary took the umbrella and immediately scurried indoors and up to the bedroom to change out of her damp clothes, leaving Tony to unload the car.

"That was quick, I thought you were going to get changed". Tony quipped as he met Mary descending the stairs. "I didn't bother after all, my dress has dried on me, I'll have a bath as soon as we've had a bite to eat". "I've left your picture, it's already been soaked once, I'll fetch it later. I'm just going to dry off". Tony said as he grabbed Mary's small holdall on his way to the bathroom. "I'm just making some sandwiches" Mary announced as Tony entered the kitchen. "I've popped your bag in your bedroom". Tony informed without admitting he'd noticed that the silver framed photograph of Mary's husband had been removed.

Mary appeared in the lounge after having her bath looking refreshed in an all cream cotton dressing gown.

Tony entered a few moments later with a fresh pot of tea. "It looks as if the rain is easing off, I'll go and fetch your picture as soon as I've drunk this tea". Tony said.

Selecting a couple of large plastic supermarket bags from a kitchen cupboard, Tony scuffed his way over the loose shingle drive. Reaching across the rear seats of the Mercedes with his back and legs exposed to the light rainy drizzle, he slid a bag over each end of the picture for protection before returning indoors.

"Before I pop off I'll put this up for you if you want me to". Tony gasped with exhaustion from running the twenty yards from his car parked in the road. "Get your breath back first". Mary requested. "You're not as fit as you think" She laughingly added. "You've not really got a spare wall". Tony noted. "Take the mirror down over the fireplace, it's a bit old fashioned anyway, it'll stop me from keep on worrying at seeing myself every time I walk in the room". Mary joked. Tony removed the mirror and fortunately the wall fixings suited the new picture stringing.

"That's lucky, that doesn't happen often, saves having to take the old hooks out". Tony said as he shuffled the picture along the stringed back until it was central and level. "Does that look about right ?" He asked. "Yes, that looks lovely, it seems bigger on the wall though".

"It's not Saint Ives, it looks more like Mouzle harbour to me". Tony suggested. "Looks nice anyway". Mary replied stepping back half way across the room to admire her new acquisition.

"Right then, I'll say goodnight, hope you've enjoyed the weekend. I'll pick you up tomorrow at two". Tony stated After a passionate kiss Mary stood in the shelter of the open doorway and watched as Tony slowly drove out of sight.

****

.

CHAPTER SEVEN

Mary lifted the receiver at the side of the bed at the same time as attempting to tidy the bedroom. "Mary, it's Susan". Came the voice from the other end of the line. "Yes I can tell your accent a mile away". Mary answered. "Bit late, I thought you said you were going to ring me three weeks ago, any problem ?" "No, sorry Mary, I should have kept you up to date.

Anyway I've booked the bus for next Monday, the third of September. It drops me in Plymouth about seven o'clock at night". "That's the day before Gillian and Robert come home. I'll meet you at the bus station. How's mum ?" Mary asked.

"No different really, me and Walter saw her on Sunday, I just wonder how much longer she's got.

Well I'll ring you from the bus when we're getting close, bye then. Remember me to the handsome Tony". "I'll make sure I keep you two a good distance apart. See you Monday". The sisters ended their conversation in fits of laughter.

Susan was standing alone besides her suitcase as Mary drove into the bus station. With a quick wave of recognition Susan swiftly strode to the parked Mercedes dragging the heavy luggage with both hands. After a sisterly hug the two ladies jointly lifted the case into the boot.

"Have you been waiting long ?" Mary asked. "The bus was a bit early, I've been here about ten minutes, that's all". Susan replied. "How was your journey ?" "Very boring after the first hour, we stopped at all the pick places all the way down.

One family got on every ones nerves. A mum,

dad and their two brats kept singing stupid songs all the while. The driver as good as threatened to throw them off. The whole bus clapped when they got off at Torquay.

Walter took me to Birmingham to catch the bus, this family was already on. It was a good job I sat down the other end".

Mary drove out of the bus station car park and for the next hour the two elegantly dressed attractive ladies, instantly recognisable as sisters with their identical slim figures and facial features chatted continuously throughout the whole journey.

Mary turned the car off the sea front and within about a hundred yards came to a halt on the shingle drive, scattering the loose chippings. Mary struggled out of the drivers door and began scooting the loose stones around with her feet.

"I regret having this drive done now". Mary moaned. "Tony said at the time to have tarmac or sets". "Where is he ?" Susan asked mischievously. "He doesn't live here with me you cheeky sod, he's got his own place, he lives about eight mikes away, you'll see him tomorrow.

Have you brought your dance shoes ?, it's our tea dance tomorrow afternoon ?"..

The telephone had been ringing for almost a minute before Mary realised and came in from the garden. "It's Gillian". Mary informed Susan, who was now standing at her side. "What's the matter Gillian, you sound upset, are you alright ?" "Robert's mother has had an accident, his uncle met us off the boat and taken Robert to the hospital". "What happened to her ? Is she badly hurt ?" "I don't know, but she's in a coma, his uncle Ron said it only happened yesterday afternoon, She fainted or had a seizure and fell getting off the bus". "Oh God, I hope she's going to be alright.

How long is it going to take you to get to the hospital ?" "I'm not with them mum, I'm stood here on Southampton station waiting for a train. I could have gone with them but I want to get home.

They dropped me off and sorted me out with a ticket, I got confused and never asked the time of the train, I'll have to go back to the booking office and find out. I'll ring you back and let you know". "Ring me as soon as you can Gillian, I'll pick you up, let me know the time it gets in".

"Who's that talking to you mum ? It's your aunt Susan, she's staying for a couple of weeks". "Hello auntie Susan, see you later, bye then".

"That didn't sound too good". Susan said having overheard the gist of the conversation with Gillian. Before Mary could reply the telephone rang again. "Mum, me again. The next train to Plymouth doesn't leave here till twenty five past three and gets me in to Plymouth about half six". "Okay then Gillian, I'll be there to meet you. You've got a couple of hours to kill, go and get yourself something to eat". "I'll let you know if Robert rings, in any case

I'll ring you again from the train when it's nearer to Plymouth. Bye mum, bye auntie Susan" Gillian shouted.

"How old is Robert's mother ?" Susan asked "I think she's just gone sixty". Mary replied. "Tony will be here at two o'clock, so lets have some lunch. I can't say I feel like dancing this afternoon, I want to wait for Gillian to ring. You still go with Tony". Mary suggested. "We'll have to see how Tony feels". Susan said hopefully.

"He reminds me of the fella who sang 'Some Enchanted Evening' in the film South Pacific, you know...Rossano Brazzi". Susan quipped, admiring a photograph of Tony on the sideboard. “He'll love you for that comparison, he's vain enough without encouragement”. Mary joked.

In anticipation that Tony would be willing to go to the dance without Mary, Susan changed into a pale green flower printed dress, and at the age of 66, together and her younger sister are both still extremely attractive women.

“You'll give the fellas a heart attack this afternoon looking like that”. Mary said with sincere admiration.

“Rossano's here”. Susan shouted excitedly. “You answer the door, that'll surprise him, but don't call him that”. Mary said.

Susan stood in the open doorway, Tony temporary stopped on the drive. He then recognised the glamorous lady waiting to greet him. “Oh hello, I remember you”. He blurted out. “You're Susan, we had a couple of dances at the wedding. Mary told me you were coming to stay soon for a holiday, she didn't tell me it was this week. Lovely to see you”.

Tony held Susan by both hands and kissed her lightly on the cheek. “Susan coming with us ?” Tony asked. “I'm not going this afternoon, I'm waiting in for a call from Gillian, then I've got to go to Plymouth again later on to meet the train”. Mary then informed Tony of the reason for her decision.

“You still go with Susan, she's been looking forward to going to the dance, she never gets a chance at home”. Susan looked at Tony and smiled as he nodded with enthusiastic approval.

“We'll be back in time, I'll drive you to the station after the dance, we'll be back by quarter to five”. “You two get off then, have a good time. I'll get dinner ready for then, and we can be away by half five.” Mary added.

With all the preparation for the early meal completed, Mary chose to relax outside in a garden chair on the patio and finish reading the morning newspaper. Almost immediately she was disturbed by the ringing of the telephone from the lounge extension.

Her irritation subsided when she realised that it was most probably Gillian calling. "Hello mum". "You alright ?" "Yes, I'm okay now, we've just left from Southampton, it's on time so I should be in Plymouth by half past six".

"Have you heard from Robert ?" "Yes, I was just going to tell you. They went straight to the hospital, she's at Guildford. He said he'd just seen her,they've brought her out of the coma. She's got some nasty cuts and bruises and he said she still seems dazed.

She can't remember what she did. The doctors intend to keep her in for the rest of the week for tests to see if they can find any reason for her to collapse".

"What's Robert going to do ?" "He's going to stay at his mum's bungalow for a few days". "Where does she live then ?" "It's a couple of miles from Woking, she's got an old people's bungalow. It used to be his grans.

After his dad left home his mum couldn't afford the mortgage where they lived and it was repossessed so she had to go and live with his gran. She died a few years ago but they allowed his mum to carry on living there".

"Sounds as though she hasn't had an easy life". Mary said with a loud sigh. "I won't have any news left to tell at this rate, see you later". Gillian whispered as she assumed passengers further along the carriage could have overheard her conversation. "I'll be waiting on the platform, bye Gillian".

"You two look as though you've had a good afternoon". Mary called out from the doorway to see

Susan and Tony laughing as they walked from Tony's car parked at the kerbside. “I really enjoyed that, smashing dance, they might nearly all be pensioners, but they know how to have a great time”. Susan enthused.

“You like our oldies tea dance then ?” Mary joked. “I absolutely loved it, I assume they're every Tuesday ?”

“She turned a few heads, soon got to know everyone. Her accent fascinated one or two of them”. Tony quipped. “That sounds like my sister. Anyway Gillian rang, her train gets in at half six. Tell me all about it later, I've laid dinner up in the dining room”. Mary said..

“I'll stay and clear up, you and Tony can get going”. Susan urged. “Are you sure you don't want to come ?” Mary enquired. “I'll be glad of the rest after yesterdays journey and the dance, go on, get going you don't want to leave Gillian waiting”.

“Susan enjoyed herself then Tony ?” “I should say so, if she wasn't dancing with me, someone else soon jumped in. I don't think she sat out one dance”. Tony replied with a laugh “There wasn't a dance she didn't do, she picked up the sequence dances after a few steps. She certainly knows how to dance”.

“That's Susan alright, she's full of energy. When we were kids mum and dad taught us to do ballroom and Latin, Susan was more keen than me and went to professional lessons for a couple of years. It's just a pity Walter's not interested”

“They all asked why you weren't there, I let them think I'd got a new woman....only kidding”. .

The Mercedes turned into the station car park. “I'll go and get a parking ticket, you carry on, it's almost time, I'll come and find you”.

An out of breath Tony joined Mary on the platform. “You okay ? You seem out of puff”. “Yes I'm fine, I ran the last bit”. The train appeared and drew into the station, doors began to spring open.

Mary scoured the length of the platform watching commuters leaving and boarding the train. “There's Gillian”. Tony announced, seeing her down at the far end looking a very lonely figure, waiting as a guard lifted her heavy luggage from the train.

First Mary and then Tony gave Gillian a hug as she joined them, leaving her suitcase where the guard had left it.. Tony quickly strode the twenty yards and returned dragging the wheeled baggage behind him.

“I didn't ask you earlier, how was your cruise ?”. Mary enquired. “Absolutely marvellous”. Gillian gushed as she flung her arms around Tony's waist and gave him an extra hug. “Thank you, that cabin was a fantastic surprise. We went ashore at all the islands, we had a wonderful time. Just a pity about hearing about Robert's mum the minute we got back”.

“I'll sit in the back with you Gillian”. Mary said, dropping the central armrest down between them, while Tony hoisted Gillian's suitcase into the boot. “Tony”. Gillian said leaning towards Tony's shoulder. “You've not asked, so I assume mum's told you why I'm on my own, Roberts not run off”, “Yes, let's hope his mother's going to be okay”.

“My junction's soon, would you like to come and stay with me and your auntie Susan until Robert gets back ?” “I'd like to go home mum, the cottage has been empty for a month now, I'm looking forward to seeing it again”.

Gillian and Robert have lived in their two bedroom end of terrace two storey cottage in a small village some six miles inland from Mary for just over two years.

Gillian chose to be married in the pretty village church with the intention of walking the short distance from her home. Only at the last possible moment did she decide to use a wedding car for fear of a forecast of rain, which proved to be wildly incorrect.

The Mercedes left the busy main road for the solitude of the quiet country lanes for the last few miles of the journey. Passing the local stores Tony travelled a further three hundred yards to reach Gillian's cottage. Gillian's neighbour immediately appeared, but before she could ask Gillian, Gillian began to explain the situation. "This is Maxine from next door, she's been looking after the house while we were away". "Yes we already met at your wedding". Tony answered. "Nice to see you again"... "There's not been any problems, it's not burnt down". Maxine said referring to Gillian's fear of thatched roofs..

"We'll just see you settled back in and we'll be off". Mary said. Tony clattered the tiny front door as he tried to lift the heavy suitcase over the threshold.

"What you got in here Gillian, the ship's anchor". Tony joked. "That's all my stuff, Robert's got the anchor in his". Gillian shouted from the kitchen. "Do you want a cup of tea before you go ?" Gillian again shouted. "No, you get yourself sorted out and I'll see you tomorrow if you'd like to come for your lunch".

"Yes I'd love to, see you in the morning then, and auntie Susan. I'll give you a ring if I hear any more news from Robert". Gillian came to the garden gate and watched as the Mercedes drove away. "Gorgeous looking young lady is Gillian, just like her mother". Tony remarked admiringly,

observing Gillian through the car rear view mirror.
"She's really special to you, isn't she ?" Mary said.

"Are you coming in for a while ?". Mary asked as the car drew up to her house. "It's a bit late. I'll get on and let you and Susan have an evening together". Tony replied.

The sound of the key in the front door caused a startled Susan to sit up from her brief nap in the armchair. "Sorry, did I wake you ?" "Just dozed off for a few minutes". An embarrassed Susan replied. "Is Gillian safely home ? I thought she might have come here for a couple of nights". "No, she wanted her own place, I can understand that". Mary answered.

"Any more news about Robert and his mother ?" Susan asked. "No, no more than you already know. Gillian's coming over tomorrow for lunch to see you". "Oh good, we can have a nice chat.

Shall I make you something to eat and drink Mary ?" "That sounds nice, I wouldn't say no, I'm starving".

"What time are you expecting Gillian". Susan asked. "Well I told her to come for lunch, so I suppose she'll be here about twelve.

Do you feel like a walk as far as Daniel's shop, it's only about fifteen minutes away". Mary asked. "Yes I'd love to, I know where it is, what do you need ?" "Only something for lunch, a packet of nice ham and some sort of salad. Debra sells those packs of mixed leaves, they'll do, I've got tomatoes". "Don't you fancy coming with me for a walk ?" "I'll wait here just in case Gillian turns up early, do you want some cash ?" "Don't be silly...I won't be long".

Susan collected a plastic carrier bag from a kitchen cupboard and screwing it up tightly in her hand, left by the rear garden gate.

Susan stood looking out of the lounge window, eagerly awaiting the arrival of Gillian's red Fiesta. At the first sighting Susan bounced down the path as Gillian crunched to a halt on the shingle drive.

Susan grabbed Gillian in a tight hug as she emerged from her car. “Hello you”. Susan gushed affectionately as they proceeded to walk hand in hand to the front door. Gillian loosed Susan's hand and stepped smartly back to her car and returned carrying a black computer.

“Our wedding photos arrived while we were away, I put them all on to the laptop”. Gillian explained and set it down on the coffee table. “I had a look at them last night, I think they're really good. See what you think”.

“Let's have lunch first, it's all ready. Don't you think Robert ought to see them before you show them to anyone else ?” Mary suggested. “He won't mind mum”.

Gillian sat in the centre of the settee, with Mary one side and Susan the other, Gillian clicked on to the first of the numerous professional photographs.

After the many admiring comments as the photographs appeared one after the other, Mary suddenly requested. “Don't go so fast Gillian, stop, go back a couple, one more, stop. Who's the young woman at the back standing next to your friend Maxine ?” “I never noticed her, I don't know who she is, she's no one Robert invited. She must have been moving, she's a bit out of focus or it's a reflection from the sun.

Strange person, I'll show Robert but I'm sure he won't know....unless it's his an old flame he's been keeping from me”. Gillian joked. “It'll all sort Itself out, somebody must know her”. Susan added.

"Doesn't matter that much anyway, we've got several group photos to choose from". Gillian said.

"I've seen the photos I'm going to have copies off, I will have another look before you order your album selection" Mary said. "I've already decided, I can tell you mine now". Susan interrupted. ""The one of you on your own at your garden gate. I think that one's beautiful, and the one of you and Robert stood on the church steps.. Oh! and of course I must have one of me and Walter, so I'll have a copy off whichever group photo you have. That's three".

Robert's not phoned again Gill ?" "Yes mum, he rang late last night from his mum's bungalow, he said he's going to stay till she's out of hospital, his uncle Ron says he'll keep an eye on her". Gillian continued. "I won't bore you with all our holiday photos, I think we've had enough, I'll show you them next time".

"Tea or coffee anyone ?" Mary asked. "Not for me mum, I need to get back, I haven't even unpacked yet, let alone done any washing".

****

.

CHAPTER EIGHT

"What on earth have you got there ?" Susan exclaimed, watching Mary enter the lounge balancing an old shoe box on top of three thick ledger like books. "I just had a bout of nostalgia after seeing Gillian's photos.

These albums must have been in the bottom of my wardrobe for the past forty years". "You're a mucky devil, look at the dust". Susan cheekily joked. "I can't remember looking at my own wedding photos since we were married,

Tony will be round this evening, give us something to do instead of staring at the tele all night". For the rest of the afternoon the sisters took a relaxing stroll along the sea shore.

"Tony's here, he's smelled the dinner cooking, he always knows what time to turn up". Mary joked. Susan opened the front door before he had chance to ring the bell or insert his key. "Hiya Susan, something smells good, it's either the food or it's you two girls". Tony shouted mischievously in the direction of the kitchen. "Cheeky sod". Mary shouted back with a loud laugh. "Get sat down and shut up, dinner's ready".

Tony was already delving through the photograph albums when Mary and Susan came into the lounge. "Where did these come from ?" Tony asked as he turned back to the beginning of Mary's wedding album.

"Gillian came round earlier for lunch, and she brought the computer to show us her wedding photos, so I just fancied having a look at mine. These albums haven't seen the light of day for over forty years. Lets start at the beginning". Mary took the album from Tony and sat besides Susan on the settee in front of the coffee table.

Turning back the fine tissue, still in excellent condition due to it not being exposed to the light for all those years, to reveal the photographs page by page. “You've never shown these to me before”. . Tony said as Susan handed the album across to him as he sat in his usual armchair. “I haven't seen them myself since we were married”. Mary quipped. “The other albums are just boring family snaps, and God knows what's in the box”. Tony moved over to the settee beside Mary, forcing Susan to inch along to make room.

With two of the albums already viewed, an obviously bored Susan emerged from the kitchen clutching three mugs of tea. “Take that one”. She urged Tony, allowing her then to place the other two mugs on the table.

Susan squeezed back on to the settee ready for the last of the albums. “Remember this holiday Susan ?”. Mary asked as she opened to the first page to reveal a set of black and white photographs.. “Oh, goodness yes, I never kept mine”. Susan replied.

Tony put his hand across the book to prevent Mary turning the page. Suddenly in an excited and trembling voice.. “**That's me**”. He gulped. “Don't be stupid”. Mary said irritated by Tony's intervention..

“These were taken in nineteen fifty eight, when me and Susan was on holiday in Swanage. That's Thomas my husband”. “I know it's Swanage, I'm not kidding. “**It is me**”. Tony repeated emphatically. Mary and Susan looked at each other in disbelief.

“You're trying to say that that's you sitting on the sea wall with your arm round my waist ?” Susan blurted out in her Birmingham accent. “Yes it is me”. Tony repeated at the same time showing his frustration at their reluctance to believe him. “**It izz me**”. Mary quickly bounced back. “How come you've never recognised Thomas then, you've seen his photo often enough ?" "I didn't know him, we only met the day before, we were both on our own.

We met at the Bridport YHA, we were paired up to do chores, in those days you were given a job to do each day. We were both biking on to Swanage the next day so we palled up. Otherwise I would never had been with him. After three nights at Swanage, I think he started back home and I remember I went on along the coast to Gosport.

So I never saw him again. I wouldn't be able to recognise him even if he'd been a friend, this was nearly fifty years ago".

"I know I gave you my address, but you never wrote, I seem to remember you promised you would". Susan chirped. "Yes I know you did but when I got back home I couldn't find it, I really did intend to write". Tony sighed.

"I wish you two would shut up, you're beginning to make me jealous". Mary joked. By now after a couple of hours of 'do you remember this' and 'do you remember that' Mary and Susan seemed almost convinced that the other lad in the photographs was Tony.

"There's a few more of that holiday and some taken after you and Thomas had gone". Mary added. Tony picked up his mug of tea and moved back to the armchair, his pulse still racing and his face feeling flushed with nervous excitement. "Well". He exclaimed. "Unbelievable...we've known each other all this time and never realised". "I'll have to ring Walter tomorrow, he'll never believe me". Susan said.

"I don't think anyone will". Mary quipped. The room went quiet as they sat and looked at each other totally bemused. "I'd love copies of those photos". Tony said breaking the silence. "And I would". Susan added.

"So...it's my sister you prefer then". Mary ribbed. "Just think, if you hadn't lost her address you two might well be married now, there's a thought". Mary sighed.

"I don't know about you two ladies but my drinks gone cold, I'm going to make afresh pot. Anybody else want one ?" Tony asked, collecting the other mugs on his way to the kitchen

. The conversation continued until almost midnight with each of them telling their various memories of those few days at the Dorset seaside town. Each memory endorsing that Tony was the other lad in the photographs on that holiday in the summer of nineteen fifty eight.

****

CHAPTER NINE

“Gillian was on the phone while you were out walking this morning”. Mary informed. “Is she okay ? What did she have to say” “Robert's coming home on Saturday, he says his mother is being let home for the weekend.

She has been given an appointment to have a scan and more tests next week. His uncle Ron is going to take care of her”. ”So they don't know why she passed out yet then ? Lets hope they don't find anything nasty, is uncle Ron her brother ?” Susan asked. “Yes, I think he lives quite close, he lost his wife very young, she was only in her early thirties when she died. He lives on his own, never remarried....Oh the odd thing Gillian said was that somehow Robert's got the idea that he was adopted, she said he sounded quite upset about it”.

“What's given him that impression ?” Susan interrupted. “Apparently while his mum's been in hospital he had a look through lots of old letters and documents, and found some reference to him being born in Horsham. His parents let him think he was born in Saint Neots where they lived at the time”.

“That's not much to go on”. Susan again interrupted. “No but he told Gillian he also found a letter from an adoption society dated nineteen eighty three referring to a baby boy, but there wasn't any name on it.

It just thanked Mister and Missis Hines for their interest and that they would be in touch within a few days”..”It doesn't mean that Robert is the baby boy in the letter”. Susan said. “Well the alternative could mean that Robert is their son and they intended to have him adopted. I doubt if he's thought of that” Mary said.

"Better keep that silly thought to yourself". Susan retorted sternly.

"After all that I completely forgot to mention the Swanage holiday and the photos, I'll ring her back later today". "There's probably a simple explanation, I can't imagine his mother wouldn't have told him by now". Susan added. "I suppose Robert has had to come back this weekend because school term starts next Tuesday". Mary stated.

Mary answered her front door to be surprised by the presence of her eldest son Thomas and his wife Elaine. "Come on in....not so warm today, I don't normally see you on a Saturday unless it's for football".

"It is football mum, it's our first match this afternoon". "I don't get to see you as often as I used to since you moved out of town". Mary said to Elaine. "No, the only real chance I get now is to come along with Thomas. We don't have a bus service, I'd have to walk almost to the next village for the nearest stop. I keep asking him to teach me to drive, some reason he's always busy, or there's something wrong with the car. So he says". Elaine replied.

"Anyway you're staying here till Thomas gets back, we can have a good old natter. Susan's here with me for another week or so, she'll be back soon, she's only popped out for a stroll. I'll tell you all about our Swanage holiday coincidence". "What's that all about then mum ?" Thomas asked.

Mary couldn't contain her eagerness "Well". She commenced, and was still describing the fascinating chain of events when Susan returned and excitedly joined in the conversation, talking over Mary and repeating details Mary had already told. "I'd love to stop and hear the rest mum, but I've got to dash".

Thomas said. "See you later". He shouted as he left through the front door. "Gillian nearly fell through the floor when I phoned her, I'm sure she didn't believe me. I haven't had chance to tell Daniel and Debra yet, I must give them a ring". Mary said.

"You and Tony have been together for a good many years now, still no thoughts of getting married ?" Elaine asked mischievously. "No..no I keep telling him we're fine the way we are, it's always in the back of my mind that my husband might one day knock on the door. It's not impossible, no one knows what happened, he might even be living another life somewhere. I wouldn't know what to do if he did come back". Mary replied painfully.

"Let's see these photos then". Elaine requested changing the subject. "Oh yes, I can see Tony in this one, with the other lad and I assume that's you Susan, sitting on the sea wall. Look at that funny expression, he still does that now when the sun's in his eyes". Elaine said with a finger pointing to the fair haired boy on Susan's left.

"I must have taken that picture. I can see what you mean, he does pull that silly face". Mary said. "Some story, Walter didn't believe me at all when I phoned him, and then he sounded a bit miffed, he pretended to be jealous. I began to get a bit worried until he started laughing and said he was only joking. I still don't know if he believes me". Susan chirped.

"Tony has a printer, so he's going to take some copies if you want a set". Mary informed. "Yes, I want a set, when I get home I'll have a search, I must still have the photos I took somewhere in the house". Susan quipped. "Me and Thomas would like a set as well" Elaine added.

"It sounds like Tom's back". Elaine remarked hearing the side gate rattle on it's hinges. "The way you treated that gate I assume you've lost". She teased as Thomas entered through the French doors. "Yes we did, four one. I'm too old for this game now, my legs have stiffened so much I'm struggling to walk, this is going to be my last season I think". "Gillian's expecting Robert home this evening, so he'll be able to play next week". Mary said sympathetically. "We certainly could have done with him today". Thomas replied.

Thomas slumped into Tony's favourite armchair as Susan laid the photograph album on his lap and opened it to reveal the first page of the clipped in monochrome prints. "Guess who that is with your future mum and dad". "That's scary, unbelievable, it can't be Tony, is it him ?" Thomas gasped. "It is". Susan said excitedly. "You know...Tony's been like a dad to me since I was about twelve. Wait till I see him again, the old devil. There he is canoodling with auntie Susan, and now my mum's his girl friend" "Less of your cheek, you're not too old to get your legs slapped". Mary joked. "Anyway Elaine we need to get going". "Another ten minutes, your mum's just made a pot of tea.

Tony arrived as usual just in time for the evening meal with Mary and Susan. "Elaine and Thomas called earlier, Elaine spent the afternoon here with me and Susan while Thomas went to play football". "Did you show the photos ?"

"They were absolutely amazed that me and Susan met you all those years and never knew. Elaine could see a likeness straight away". Susan lifted the nearest telephone extension. "Hello auntie Susan, is mum there ?" "Just a minute Gill, Mary it's Gillian for you". "Everything alright Gillian". Mary asked. "Yes, just ringing to let you know Robert's home, we've just got in, I picked him up from

Liskeard station". "How is he ? Is his mum any better ?" "He's okay, still muttering on about being adopted though. He says she looks a lot better, still feels shaken up.

We're going to nip to the pub for something to eat first, then when we come back home Robert wants to have a look at the wedding photos. I told him all about you and Susan just finding out you'd known Tony fifty years ago when you were teenagers on holiday".

"I bet he didn't believe you, anyway you get on then". Mary replied. "We'll have a ride over tomorrow, I'll bring the laptop again, you can show me exactly which photos you want, and auntie Susan. We'll be over after lunch mum", "We'll see you tomorrow then, bye Gillian". Mary returned the handset back to it's base in the lounge and proceeded to inform Susan and Tony the substance of the telephone conversation.

****

CHAPTER TEN

Mary and Susan stood chatting in the front garden with Mary's neighbour when a smiling Gillian steered her red Fiesta between the entrance pillars and gently rolled forward on to the drive. Robert and Gillian followed Mary through the rear gate into the lounge via the French doors, leaving Susan still in deep conversation with the neighbour.

"Susan's having a job to get away from Missis Parker, bit naughty of us to leave her there on her own". Gillian laughed. "It serves her right, she's the one who keeps the chat going, I feel sorry for Beryl. She's still telling all about knowing Tony all those years ago". Mary replied. "Make yourselves comfortable, I'll make a drink". Mary added.

"At last you're back Susan, I've left you a cup of tea in the pot, see if it's still hot". "That neighbour of yours can't half rattle, I couldn't get away, you rotten devils didn't care, leaving me there". Susan grunted. "It sounded to me that you was the one doing all the talking, I was beginning to feel sorry for Beryl". Mary joked with both sisters laughing. Susan ditched the tea pot and quickly made herself a fresh mug of coffee. "I'll have a look at those holiday photos of you two with Tony later". Robert shouted from the lounge.

"Has Robert thought any more about this adoption business ?" Mary whispered to Gillian. "What you two whispering about ?" Robert asked sharply. "I was just telling mum that you hadn't decided whether to do anything yet. You're still not sure if you were adopted, you're only guessing at the moment". "No I'm not". Robert insisted. "I know I'm right, I just don't understand why mum never told me. I intend to ring uncle Ron later, he obviously knows". "If you are right, your mum probably thought it was best to leave well alone once your dad left home". Mary said sympathetically.

"Anyway let's have another look through your wedding photos, and your honeymoon pictures". "Robert didn't recognise that woman in that group photo". Gillian said. "She's no one that I invited, I've never seen her before". Robert confirmed. "She's not on any of the other photos, so I guess someone invited her on, or her mates have put her up to it for a dare, forget it. It's a poor photo anyway. We've got several other group photos to choose from". He added.

"Have you got a price list Gillian ? We can see how much me and Susan owe you now we've finally chosen".

Another hour passed by, viewing the seemingly hundreds of honeymoon photographs, including an enthusiastic verbal description of each picture by Gillian as it appeared on the screen.

"My eyeballs are aching". Susan chipped in jokingly. "I've had enough as well, I've already seen them a couple of times". Robert added sarcastically. "You rotten pair". Gillian responded in a mocked angry voice.

"You two are both back to work next week then ?" Mary asked "Yes, I've got a new intake of little ones to teach". Gillian sighed.

"Thomas and Elaine were here yesterday". Mary said. "We lost our first match, he rang me last night, I'll see him at training Tuesday evening". Robert replied.

"How long are you staying auntie Susan ?" Gillian asked. "Another week, I'm going back a week tomorrow". "That's alright then, we'll definitely see you again before you go". "We're going to get off now mum".

"Don't you want to stop and have some dinner ?" "We would love to mum, but we've arranged to see some friends in the pub this evening. It's one of Robert's college mates and his wife, they came to our wedding evening".

"What did you reckon to our tea dance this afternoon ?" Tony asked Susan as they sat at the dining table enjoying the roast beef meal Mary had prepared. "I loved it, pity it's my last one, I don't think I sat out a single dance". "We did notice, where the hell do you get the energy ?" Mary commented with a laugh.

"One chap I danced with asked me to go dancing on Friday night. I said I'd think about it, but he must have changed his mind by the end of the dance because he never asked me again. He said his name was Joe, tall chap with white hair, he sat in a group next to the keyboard player".

"He probably realised that a whole nights dancing with you would kill him. That's Joe Angwin, he is seventy nine, and he probably wants to see eighty , so that's why he thought better of it". Mary joked.

Tony craftily slid away to the comfort of his armchair in the lounge while Mary and Susan continued their chatter as they cleared the dining room and tidied the kitchen.

"Notice Rossano Brazzi has sneaked off again". Susan joked very quietly. "Where is this Friday night dance ?" Susan enquired. "Well it's not round here, nothing happens here any night, he must be going in to Plymouth I'd imagine". Mary replied.

From the sea front Mary could see Gillian's red Fiesta standing on her drive as she and Susan returned from their stroll along the beach. Gillian and Robert were both waiting on the pavement leaning against the garden wall. “You two been waiting long ?” Mary asked. “Only about ten minutes”. Gillian replied. “Your Thomas is here now”. Susan chipped in as they watched his car come to a halt blocking the access to the drive. “Robert's meeting Tom here”. Gillian quickly explained. “Hi everyone”. Thomas called out as he clambered from his tired looking Jaguar, a candidate for a classic car if it was restored. “You fit young Robert ? Right then lets get going and see what we can do this Saturday”.

Robert slung his holdall across the rear seats and settled into the front passenger seat. “We'll see you girls later”. Thomas shouted as the car moved away and turned right on reaching the sea front. “You girls”. Susan repeated. “Cheeky devil”.

“It's too nice to sit inside”. Mary suggested. Susan and Gillian laid out the garden loungers on the sunny patio while Mary was busy preparing sandwiches and a tray of tea. “Has Robert found out any more ? Did he ring his uncle ?” Mary asked Gillian. “Not yet, he doesn't want to put him on the spot, I think he'd prefer to speak to his mum first. He's certain that he was adopted from a letter he found at his mum's”.

“I shouldn't really say this.....but don't you think it's possible his mum and dad are his real parents and they were considering having him adopted, you don't know what their situation was at the time. What ever you do, don't say anything to Robert, I'm probably completely wrong, it's just a thought”. Mary said, with immediate regret. “I'd never thought of that, surely not”. Gillian said now shocked into silence.

“What's Robert going to do next ?” Mary asked attempting to lighten the mood. “He went on the internet and ordered a birth certificate last night from the West Sussex registry office". "How can he do that, his surname would have been different on his original birth certificate ?" Mary asked.

"He's pretty sure he was born in hospital in Horsham, so he used that and his date of birth and his full name. He hopes his Christian names Robert Stewart haven't changed. He told them his surname is his adopted name, so he thinks they'll look for an alternative knowing all the other information".

"That all sounds reasonable, let's hope he gets something back from them soon". Mary said. "I hope so, he's driving me mad with it, he never thinks about anything else at the moment". Gillian added.

"Whatever you do, for goodness sake don't mention what I said, I shouldn't have suggested it". Mary urged.

"You've not said a lot auntie Susan". "It's not my business. I told you...Mary... to keep that to yourself. I do hope it all turns out okay for him".

"Are you looking forward to going home auntie Susan ?" "Not really, I've had a great time, I'll miss the beach and the dancing. I think Walter's getting a bit bored. I've had a lovely holiday, you're very lucky to live in such a beautiful place".

"Have you never thought of moving to the coast ?" Gillian asked. "I've dreamt about it, that's about all I can do, we could never do it. We couldn't afford it, what our house is worth wouldn't buy us a beach hut down here, then there's your gran, and I would have a hell of a time prizing Walter away from the love of his life".

"What's that ?" Gillian quipped. "Bloomin Aston Villa, he'd stand at the ground all day and watch the grass grow if they'd let him". Susan said annoyingly.

"That sounds like the boys are back". Susan remarked referring to the noisy banter coming from the other side of the front door. “Well....how did you get on ?” Gillian enquired sarcastically, holding the door open as they carried on ribbing each other on into the lounge.

“Well we didn't loose, two two”. Robert said proudly. “Weren't the other team a lot of good then ?” Gillian added with a grin. “We could do with a drink, mum”. Thomas stated, Ignoring Gillian's sarcasm.

“How awful, I completely forgot to ask about Robert's mum's tests last week”. Mary said apologetically. “She didn't go, the hospital put them off till next week. Apparently the consultant dealing with mum had some emergency, so she's going next Tuesday now”. Robert advised.

“We're going to leave you now mum, bye auntie Susan, see you next time, have a good journey, give my love to gran when you see her”. “Tom”. Robert called out. “Are you staying on ? Your car's across the drive”. “No, I'm off now anyway, I won't be a minute”. Thomas answered. “Bye mum, see you soon Susie”. Thomas quipped.

“I'll give you Susie”. Susan replied with a loud laugh. Mary and Susan stood on the pavement waving as first Thomas and then Gillian's car went from view.

“Three gone, now another ones turned up, just heard Tony's car crunch on the drive. I'll get the door”. Susan said rising from the comfortable armchair. “For goodness sake Susan, sit down, he'll let himself in, he's got a key”. “Evening young ladies, what are we having for dinner tonight ?” “Do you feed him every day ?” Susan joked. “We eat together almost every night, he takes me out to dinner a lot, he more than pays his share. I can't complain”. Mary said in Tony's defence.

“I'm only teasing, I know you've got a great bloke in Tony”. Susan muttered slightly apologetically.

“You'll have me blushing in a minute”. Tony chirped. “Anyway, forgetting how fantastic I am, here's the photo copies of Swanage, I've printed four complete sets”. “I still can't believe that's you after all these years” Susan said.

All three were now relaxing, slowly digesting the evening meal. Susan seated in an armchair clutching her set of prints in one hand and a copy a of the Peoples Friend laid open on her lap as tiredness overcame her, and as her eyes slowly closed the photographs slipped from her hand onto the open magazine. Meantime, Tony looked across at Mary and nodded in the direction of Susan and smiled as he hopped around the television channels.

Mary wandered to the desk in the hallway and returned with her tatty looking note pad. Putting her feet up and stretching out on the settee with a set of Tony's prints of that holiday of fifty years ago resting on the open pad, the memories of those few days in nineteen fifty eight appeared as clear as if it was only yesterday.

Eagerly she entered everything she could remember, scribbling frantically for half an hour and filling a further three A4 pages of information towards her eventual story.

Looking across the room, the television was showing a shopping channel. Tony had nodded off in his favourite armchair with Susan fast asleep in the other.

'Thanks for the company you two' Mary thought as she tip toed between the coffee table and the armchairs to retrieve the remote control from Tony's loose grip and returned to slouch full length back onto the settee.

Mary gently tapped Susan on the shoulder. “Wake up, bed time”. Susan opened her eyes and with a dazed expression asked. “Where's Tony ?” “He went home half an hour ago, it's well past midnight. I've made you a hot drink so drink up and lets go to bed”. Mary urged. “Will I see Tony again before I leave ?” Susan asked desperately. “He'll be coming here tomorrow evening and I daresay we'll have our usual stroll to the pub”.

“Are you ready ?” Mary shouted from the foot of the stairs. “I'm coming”. Susan replied closing the bathroom door behind her. “Do you need your sun hat ? I'm wearing mine”. Mary announced as she posed in front of the hall mirror arranging the stylish straw hat on her head. “No, I'll be okay, my hair's quite thick. I detest wearing hats at the best of times”.

A few minutes walk and the sisters reached the sea front and clumsily negotiated the two feet drop onto the sandy beach. “It's a good job there's no one at this end of the beach to see that brilliant performance”. Mary said as they laughed at each other.

“What a lovely peaceful Sunday morning”. Susan remarked looking eastward towards the town. “This is how I prefer it, out of season, nice and quiet. Just as sunny but a bit cooler though, still, can't have it all ways”. Mary replied.

“I'll have to see if I can get down here again before Christmas, if you'll have me”. “Of course you're welcome, it'd be nice if Walter can come with you, we can get him dancing”. Mary joked.

The little town centre is set back from the sea front nestling behind a row of brightly painted terraced guest houses. Beyond lays an almost empty rundown amusement arcade bellowing out pop music.

Mary and Susan ventured a short distance along the High Street and entered a smart looking cafe. Mary removed her hat as they sat at a pleasant window table.

A very attractive young waitress hovered around discreetly, waiting for a sign that her services were required. “Good morning ladies”. She greeted with a friendly smile. “What would you like ?” “We'll have a pot of tea for two please”. Mary requested. “You having something to eat Susan ?” “Why not, I think I'll have a slice of that Victoria sponge”. Susan said pointing to the display of cakes laid out on the sweet trolley. “Make that two slices then please”. Mary ordered. The waitress dispensed with her note pad, returning it to her apron pocket. “Only be a moment ladies”.

“That was very nice, thank you”. Mary told the waitress at the same time leaving a small tip on the way out, stepping outside into the warmth of the morning sunshine. “Is my hat on straight ?” Mary asked while looking at her reflection in the cafe window.

“We must call in on Daniel and Debra on the way back so that I can say cheerio”. Susan said sadly.

Within ten minutes Mary and Susan entered the sea front corner shop. “Oh, hello”. Debra shouted as her last customer had just been served.

“We heard all about you two and Tony, fancy not knowing you'd met fifty years ago, and you even married the other lad. Sounds unbelievable”. Debra gushed excitedly. “Susan told us all about it”.

“When Tony suddenly said 'that's me' I thought, here we go with one of his stupid jokes, then I could see he meant it when he started to get a bit angry with me and Susan.

We didn't get to bed that night till well after

midnight, then I didn't sleep a wink, I couldn't stop thinking about it". Mary replied. "And we haven't stopped talking about since". Susan chirped. "You can probably dine out on that story for years". Debra joked.

Daniel appeared from the storeroom. "Hello mum, auntie Susan, you off home tomorrow ?" "Yes, sadly, end of a lovely holiday". Susan answered.

Mary, Susan and Daniel moved away from the counter to allow Debra to serve some more customers as a small queue began to form.

Daniel listened intensively to Susan reliving the Swanage story all over again, in every detail, especially that she was Tony's girl friend for a few days.

Mary disappeared to the rear of the stores to collect her Sunday newspaper leaving Susan to say her goodbyes.

"I'll have to ask you for a plastic bag to carry this paper". Mary remarked referring to the volume and weight of the newspaper with it's additional weekly magazines and other unwanted items as she handed a five pound note to Debra.

Debra and Daniel accompanied Mary and Susan out of the shop and onto the pavement. Mary walked slowly a few paces away as Daniel and Debra both gave Susan a hug.

The sisters crossed the road and staying on the promenade they continued their stroll back to Mary's house.

"I think that's enough walking for today". Mary proclaimed on seeing her house a short distance away. Tony and Susan lagged a few yards behind deep in conversation. "You two do realise, that walk to and from the pub was a good five miles ? on top of the couple of miles we walked this morning".

Mary added.

"Are you coming in for a while ?" Mary asked Tony. "No, I think I'll head off, it's quite late, I've said my goodbye to Susan". But before climbing into his Mercedes he gave Susan another emotional hug and a kiss on her cheek. "Have a safe journey and I'll see you again soon. I still can't believe we kissed and cuddled fifty years ago".

Susan looked quite upset as Mary left her standing alone on the pavement. Tears began to trickle down her cheeks as she continued waving and watching as Tony drove towards the sea front and out of sight.

Mary looked on as Susan climbed onto the bus and sat in the front window seat. The bus driver lifted the several items of luggage into the hold as the remaining passengers filed aboard.

The automatic doors closed. Mary waited until the bus departed the station before returning to her car to begin the journey home.

The solitude of the drive home from Plymouth allowed Mary to relive the events of the past two weeks, and her thoughts returned to the black and white Swanage holiday snapshots.

She began to imagine the outcome if Susan had dated Thomas and she Tony during that brief three day romance fifty years ago.

Would Thomas have been knocking on their door for her sister instead of her ? And would she have ever kept in touch with Tony ?

Although she adored Susan she couldn't prevent a slight feeling of envy at the attention she'd received during her stay. In particular with reference to the discovery that she was Tony's date on that holiday, and the affection Tony displayed towards her.

Mary's focus was suddenly brought back to the present through a lapse in concentration when she narrowly avoided an accident. The slow moving queue of traffic suddenly came to a halt with Mary's mind wandering, causing her to brake hard and stop within inches of a large lorry.

Mary was relieved to safely reach home and delighted to find Tony waiting in the open doorway.

****

CHAPTER ELEVEN

"Susan must have made an impression at the last two dances, nearly everyone wanted to know when she'll be coming again". Tony remarked. "No more than the impression she made on you, I think if she'd stayed any longer I would have begun to get worried". Mary replied with a nervous laugh.

"You are joking of course ?" Tony asked. "You should know me well enough by now" He added.. "No I'm pulling your leg, I haven't any worries, we've been together too long and after all we do have our special secret. I know how unfair it's been on you all these years and what you've missed. Lets get the rest of these dishes washed up". Mary said.

"Mary". Tony shouted. "It's Gillian on the phone". Mary scurried down the stairs and into the lounge. Tony dropped into his favourite armchair and searched amongst the cushions for the remote control. "Yes Gillian". "Did auntie Susan get away alright yesterday ?"

"Yes, she phoned me last night, said wished she was still down here. How's Robert's mum ?" "Robert's uncle took her in to hospital this morning, Robert's waiting for him to ring back". Gillian paused for a moment. "Robert had a reply to his application for his birth certificate this morning. It says they cannot help him as he needs to obtain his adoption file". "How does he do that ?"

"They say he has to visit the Government web site on line. He's been looking at it for the last half an hour, he must have got fed up, he's just said sod it and closed the laptop". "I can hear Robert muttering on, what's he on about ?" Mary asked. "Oh something about seeing the adoption records adviser and something about a councillor, I haven't got a clue what he's talking about. The mood he's in, I'm not going to ask". Gillian said with a stifled giggle. "You'd better let him get on with it, let me know how he gets on, and any news about his mum when he hears from his uncle". Tony held the television on mute, waiting as Mary returned the handset to it's base. Mary then attempted to accurately tell Tony the interesting parts of Gillian's call.

"He might as well just bite the bullet and ask his uncle Ron outright and be done with it, he'd probably get all he needs to know from him. His uncle obviously knows all about it". Tony said in an authoritarian manner. "He can't really mention it to his mum at the moment". He added. "Well it's not up to us to interfere, it's Robert's business. Anyway is there anything worth watching, put the sound back up". Mary instructed.

The next morning Mary made her routine weekly visit to the nearest supermarket about three miles away situated on an area resembling an industrial estate, several other large well know stores also occupy the site.

Mary left the supermarket pushing the out of control shopping trolley at an awkward angle in an attempt to steer a straight path across the busy car park back to her Mercedes. The boot lid began to rise as she approached the car. With the shopping securely stowed away and the trolley located in it's designated shelter ready for the next unsuspecting shopper, Mary sighed with relief as she drove from the car park after purchasing the groceries for another week.

The mobile telephone in Mary's handbag resting on the passenger seat rang for several seconds before ringing again for a further twenty seconds or so. Mary eventually found a convenient flat section of roadside verge to draw to a halt. “Hello mum, I assume you're probably driving, ring me when you can, something to tell you”, The voice mail announced. Mary's curiosity made her reply immediately, but this time it was Gillian's voice mail that answered the call. Having decided that Gillian was most likely back in class teaching, Mary rejoined the lane and completed the short journey home.

After several attempts to contact her daughter during the afternoon without success Mary's telephone began to ring. Mary hurried from the kitchen to the nearest handset in the lounge. “Gillian, I've been trying to get you, I got your message this morning”. “Yes, I was on my lunch break I've been in class all afternoon”. “What did you want to tell me ?” Mary asked with eager anticipation.

“Robert's mum had a scan yesterday and they found she has a brain tumour”. “Oh my goodness”. Mary sighed. “The news is good though, it's not malignant and the position it's in makes it possible to be removed. Still not nice, but his uncle said the consultant was very confident about the surgery”.

“Are they going to do it right away ?” “Tomorrow all being well”. “How's Robert ?” “He's very worried, but he's feeling relieved to have the consultant's assurance that she's going to be alright. Anyway, the other thing mum, he mention the adoption to his uncle.......Something else I'll tell you in a minute”.

Mary could sense Gillian was bursting at the seams with excitement about something. “His uncle was a bit reluctant to say much about it. He more or less admitted that he had been adopted but preferred that Robert speak to his mum when she's better. He did say that his mum always intended to tell him but with all the ill treatment and trouble his adopted father had inflicted, she never managed to find the right moment and by the time he'd left school and came to Cornwall she was too scared, probably thought she'd left it too late". "Let's hope Robert understands, so sad, some ones going to be upset I imagine". Mary replied.

There was a short pause in the conversation, Mary could hear the rustle of paper as Gillian was removing a letter from it's envelope. "This is the astonishing thing". Gillian said bubbling with emotion.

"Robert had a letter this morning....he's got a sister !". "What on earth are you talking about Gillian ?" "It's true, he has, he's got a sister". Gillian repeated emphatically. "He has, this letter is about her". "Go on then, what did Robert have to say ?" "He doesn't know yet, he'd gone before the post this morning".

"Don't you think you should have left the letter for him to open ?" "Goodness no, we always open each others letters. Stop interrupting mum and let me tell you what it says". "Alright I'm listening". Mary replied indignantly.

"It's from a company called Worldwide Search Limited". Mary again interrupted. "Haven't you tried phoning him ?" ""You've done it again mum, course I have, but I know he leaves his phone switched off most of the day while he's teaching, and the school team have a match after school this afternoon so he's going be late home".

Gillian paused again, took a deep breath and not hiding her frustration. "I'll start again. It's from a company called Worldwide Search Limited, They say that over the past year they have been carrying out a search on behalf of Jane Barnes and have obtained conclusive information that Robert Stewart Hines is her brother. It goes on to say she wishes to meet Robert. The letter says they will understand if he declines or he needs time to decide. It goes on to say for him to contact a John Ryalls for a discussion".

"This seems too much of a coincidence. He's just found out himself that he was adopted....think about it Gillian. It looks a bit suspect". Mary said. "Well I think it's genuine, why would anyone pretend to be his sister ? He's not famous and he's certainly got no money, so what could she be after ?" "I think it is just a pure coincidence". Gillian responded robustly. "Well if it is genuine he's got something he didn't have before...a new surname". Mary quipped.

"I'll try to get hold of Robert again when school's over". "You will ring me as soon as you can ?, let me know what Robert thinks about his letter". Mary asked. "It might be tomorrow now mum". "Okay then Gillian, don't forget to let me know as soon as he hears how his mum's operation went".

"We'll be round Saturday lunchtime anyway, I'll bring the letter, you can read it for yourself. Bye mum". Mary returned the the telephone to it's base and dropped with exhaustion on to the settee.

The sound of the front door opening brought Mary to her feet. "You in the lounge ?" Tony shouted, pushing open the lounge door. "Were you asleep ?" "Not far from it". Mary muttered.

"You'll never guess what Gillian told me earlier". "What's that then ?" Tony enquired. "She said Robert's had a letter from some genealogists telling him that he's got a sister he never knew about, and she wants to know if he'll meet her".

"You are joking" Tony quipped. "Gillian's taking it seriously, she got very excited telling me". "What's Robert had to say ?" "He didn't know then, he hadn't finished school. He left before the postman came and Gillian can't get him on his mobile, he must be home by now. I'll give Gillian a chance to ring me, she said she would as soon as Robert's read it".

"It all sounds a bit strange to me, with Robert just finding about his adoption, seems too much of a coincidence". Tony said with a hint of disbelief. "That's exactly what I suggested to Gillian, but she thinks it's genuine". Mary replied.

"Don't you think Robert will be a bit annoyed with Gillian for opening his letter, never mind that we know all about it even before he's had chance to read it himself ?" Tony asked. " I said that to Gillian, but she said they always open each others letters". "I know I'd be mad as hell if I was Robert". Tony said sharply.

"Robert spoke to his uncle last night about his mum, it's not good news, she has a tumour on the brain, but it's benign and they can remove it. They're operating tomorrow". "Wow, that doesn't sound very nice, I bet that was a surprise. Still it's a good job they've found it and can take it away. Let's hope the operation's a success". Tony said.

"Apparently the surgeon more or less assured his uncle she'd be okay". Mary replied and added. "He asked his uncle what he knew about his adoption. He didn't tell him any details about the actual adoption, he suggested that Robert ought to speak to his mother when she's better. He did say his mother will be very upset that he found out and she hadn't told him".

"With what's happened this afternoon I've not started to cook anything yet Tony, do you fancy the chip shop ?" "That'll do me, I'll nip out now if you're ready to eat. Usual ?" "Yes, I'll set up while you're gone".

Mary anxiously grabbed the telephone before it could ring a second time. "Mum". "Yes Gillian, how's

Robert, has he read his letter ?" "He hasn't put it down yet, he keeps reading it over and over again". "What does he think about it ?" Mary asked. "He's very excited at the thought of having a sister but he's not sure about it, he's a bit sceptical. He'd love it to be true". "Is he going to meet her ?"

"He wants to be certain about her first. I told him what you said about the surname so he's going to apply again for his birth certificate and put Barnes as his name and this time not mention anything about adoption". Gillian replied.

"That should be interesting, he's not bothering about the other thing ? the adoption advisory council he was looking at". Mary asked. "No, not yet, not now he's got this name. If nothing comes of it I daresay he will".

Tony replaced the handset in the hall and rejoined Mary in the kitchen. "You heard all that Tony ? What do you think ?" "Well it all sounds very interesting, I just hope Robert's not in for a big disappointment. I suppose it's worth a try, if it does get him his birth certificate then the letter would seem to be genuine.....lets hope".

"Pop the fish and chips on to plates and stick them in the microwave for a couple of minutes each". Mary instructed Tony while she made a fresh pot of tea. After a couple of "pings" Mary and Tony finally sat to enjoy their evening meal.

****

CHAPTER TWELVE

Thomas sat nursing a mug of coffee with his elbows on Mary's pine kitchen table listening intently to Mary's version about Robert's possible new sister and his latest adoption situation when the door bell rang. “That'll be them now”. Mary said. Robert marched through the hallway beaming with excitement, with Gillian on his heels anxiously trying to be the first to tell the news. “Robert's got his birth certificate, it came this morning”. She blurted out. “Go on then.....what's it say ?” Mary asked urgently. Gillian again jumped in first preventing Robert from speaking. “It must be his, everything's good, place, name and date of birth, it all checks”.

“I'll have to see it later, come on Robert, we'll have to go, we're meant to be at the ground for half one. It's about an hours bus ride today”. Thomas urged.

“It's great news about his mum”. Mary stated. “Oh yes, it couldn't have gone better according to his uncle. She'll be in intensive care for about a week”. “Is Robert going to see her ?” “Yes, he's already spoken to his headmaster, he's going Tuesday morning and coming back on Friday all being well”.

“Can I see his birth certificate ?” Mary asked Gillian. “I've got the letter here as well”. Gillian produced the photocopy of the document and handed it to Mary. Mary unfolded the A4 size sheet of paper and casting her eyes from left to right to observe the type written columns.

When and Where born.... *Tenth of January 1983 Flat 7 Eldridge Ct. Horsham* Name if Any....... *Robert Stewart* Sex.......*Boy* Name and Surname of Father.........*Thomas Barnes*

Name and Maiden Surname of Mother....... *Katherine Jane Stewart* Rank or Profession of Father............*Not Known* Signature, Description and Residence of Informant.........*K.J.Stewart Mother Flat 7 Eldridge Court Jules Eldridge Close Horsham* When Registered........*Thirty first of January 1983* Signature of Registrar......*Herbert Lockhart*

Gillian passed Robert's letter from the genealogists to Mary. Still holding the birth certificate she carefully read the letter a couple of times before returning the papers to Gillian. “The birth certificate seems to tie up with the letter, looks as though this girl is genuine. What's Robert intending to do now ?” Mary asked. “He's convinced she is his sister, so he's going to contact this Worldwide company on Monday. He's wondering now why they haven't mentioned anything about their parents”. “I bet he's feeling a bit nervous about meeting her. The letter doesn't give that much information”. Mary noted. “I think he's excited to find out if he has any other relations, he's talked about nothing else since he read the letter. Not even his football”. Gillian said. “Has he told his uncle ?” “He rang and told him, his uncle said he didn't know anything about it, he said he was surprised”. Gillian replied.

“What time are you expecting Tony, mum ?” “Oh not until seven”. “We'll probably be gone by then. You've got plenty to talk about now”. “Where are they playing today ?” Mary asked Gillian. “At Saint Austell”. “They're not going to get back from there before seven”. Mary advised

.

The jovial banter of the three men talking football on the front step got Gillian out of the comfort of an armchair to answer the door. “Sounds as though you could have won for a change". "You needn't appear surprised we won three nil". Robert said with great satisfaction. "We played well today, they'd won their first three games. Another win will get us half way up the league". Thomas added.

"You all turned up at the same time then". Mary stated. "Gillian, I've pulled onto the drive, but I'm to the side of you so you're okay for getting out". Tony advised. Then turning his attention to Robert. "How you getting on ? How's your mum ?" "She's doing well, she should be out of intensive care by the weekend. I'm going up to see her on Tuesday". "That's good news, what's happening with your sister situation ?" Tony asked. "Robert retrieved the letter and his birth certificate from Gillian's handbag and handed them to Tony. "Well I must say I was a bit sceptical about her, but this all seems pretty genuine, what do you intend to do now ?" "I don't think it's worth ringing over the weekend, so I'm going to speak to this John Ryalls bloke on Monday to see about a meeting". Robert replied. "I'm off now mum, cheerio everybody, I'll see you next Saturday Robert, let us know you'll be available, just in case you decide to stay with you mum". Thomas shouted as he closed the front door.

Gillian eventually managed to interrupt Tony and Robert's conversation. "It's time we went as well Robert, mum needs to get a meal".

Mary returned to the kitchen after seeing Gillian and Robert drive away. "Robert said something interesting when we were chatting earlier. He was on about the woman on the wedding group photo. He wondered whether she could have been his sister". Mary said. "I suppose it could have been her but why didn't she say anything, and then why did she just vanish ?" Tony added.

****

CHAPTER THIRTEEN

Mary watched the rain running down the lounge windows waiting for Tony to collect her for the afternoon tea dance. Prompt as usual at exactly two o'clock the Mercedes pulled up across the drive.

With an umbrella to hand Tony reached the front door as Mary stepped out and under it's cover. “Looks like we've seen the last of the Summer”. Tony grunted as he opened the passenger door.

“Has Gillian rung ?” “She rang me ever so early this morning, she'd just dropped Robert off at Liskeard and phoned before she went on to school.

She said Robert rang the genealogist company yesterday afternoon as soon as he got home. They are now going to let her know that Robert has agreed to meet her, but she actually lives in Italy, she lives in Rome”.

“That's going to be a bit inconvenient, who's going to visit who ? Let's hope she's able to come to England without too much trouble because I can't see how Robert can afford to make many trips to Rome”. Tony chuntered.

Les the keyboard player was stood by his instrument chatting to a well dressed young couple as Tony placed a ten pound note on his table.

“Here's two of my faithful long suffering regulars”. Les said as he introduced Tony and Mary to the new arrivals. “Nice to have some new faces, especially young ones”. Tony replied. “This is Rhona and I'm James”. “Are you staying in the hotel ?” Mary enquired. “No, we've recently moved down here from Bristol, We've bought a house about eight miles away, towards Plymouth. It's in need of a bit of work but it was the nearest to my new job we could afford". "What do you do then James ?" Tony asked. "I finally qualified as an architect a year ago and I was offered this job in Plymouth, I've been travelling back and forward until we moved into this place three months ago. Life's a lot easier now, except Rhona's getting bored, she hasn't found a job yet".

"Anyway lets go to our table, would you two like to sit with us ?" Mary asked as they strolled across the centre of the dance floor. "If you're sure you don't mind, that would be very nice, thank you". Rhona replied. "We know what it's like to be somewhere new where everybody knows each other, it always seems a bit cliquey" Mary added. "I hope you won't be disappointed this afternoon, we need some new blood, we old ones are dying off by the week. We're nearly all well past our sell buy date". James and Rhona politely laughed at Tony's feeble attempt at a joke.

"I think we ought to have this dance". Tony said as Les began to play another waltz. James and Rhona followed on to the edge of the floor. "Don't expect any fancy steps from us, we've only had a few lessons". James said nervously. "Don't worry, it's not 'Strictly', there's no stars here, you'll find everybody very friendly". Mary replied assuringly

"That's another dance over". Tony uttered as the dancers gradually deserted the ballroom. "What did you think of the afternoon you two ?" Tony asked. "I thought it was wonderful, I was petrified when we first went on the floor, especially when we got in a mess and bumped into a couple. But they just laughed and chatted to us, they were lovely. The afternoon fled by". Rhona replied. "We'll see you next week then ?" Mary asked. "All being well. If we're not here it won't be because we didn't want to come, I might not be able to get every Tuesday off work. But I thought it was a great afternoon". James said enthusiastically. "Looks like we'll be practising in the lounge tonight to sort out our cha cha routine". James added with a laugh. "Me and Tony had a sneaky peak at you and you danced very nicely together". "That's sweet of you Mary, I'm just glad we didn't embarrass ourselves". Rhona said.

"There's no need to worry here, it's all social fun, we're all pretty average dancers, some of us more useless than others". Tony joked as he stared at Mary. "Now that's not true, Mary's a lovely dancer". Rhona said with a smile. "Anyway we hope to see you next week, bye for now". Mary responded.

The ground was still wet from the earlier rain, Mary and Tony skipped around the isolated puddles lying on the surface as they crossed the car park to Tony's Mercedes. "Robert must have seen his mother by now, Gillian dropped him off at the station at seven this morning". Mary stated. Tony proceeded out of the car park and in the opposite direction to normal. "Where're we going ?" Mary asked. "To my place, I'm cooking you dinner tonight for a change, but I might need a bit of help". "A bit of help". Mary chuntered sarcastically.

After about a twenty minute drive through a series of narrow country lanes the Mercedes turned through a gap in the very high hedgerow and entered the two hundred yards long private asphalt driveway leading to an imposing double bay fronted two storey Victorian property. The private drive was isolated on either side by a timber ranch style fence enclosing a sheep grazing pasture on the right with half a dozen horses roaming the field opposite..

"I do like the new carpet". Mary noted as she passed from the hallway to the lounge. "They came and fitted it yesterday afternoon. The carpet they took up was the original carpet from when my parents moved in, so I think it probably did needed changing". "It was getting a bit threadbare, the floor boards were beginning to show". Mary laughed.

Mary kicked off her shoes at the lounge door before entering and settling down in an authentic looking reproduction red leather wing backed Queen Anne chair, while Tony vanished into the kitchen leaving the door slightly open.

"It's a bit quiet in there, are you alright ?" Mary shouted. "You couldn't give me a hand ?, I could do with some help". Mary tutted loudly as she rose from her chair. "I knew I'd end up in here, what do you want me to do ? What's that in the oven ?" Mary asked spying a long glass oven dish covered with tin foil. "Never you mind, that's the chef's special. Will you wash and do the salad ? While I make the pudding, I mean the sweet". "Pretentious sod". Mary said with a laugh. "Your salad's all ready, I hope that's what you wanted, I've laid it out on this fancy plate I'll leave you to it, I'm going back in the lounge, call me when dinner's ready. Where's the remote ?"

After a further thirty minutes Tony stood in the kitchen doorway and invited Mary into the dining room. "My goodness, this all looks wonderful, you've pushed the boat out, posh table cloth, best crockery and it looks like your parents silver cutlery". "So far so good, I just hope it tastes as good as it looks". Tony said anxiously.

The view from the dining table through the French doors to the rear garden and the surrounding farmland attracted Mary's attention. "Haven't you ever thought of moving to somewhere less lonely ? Your nearest neighbour is just about visible on a clear day". "That's the next thing, I was going to wait till we'd finished and back in the lounge". Before Tony could continue, Mary interrupted. "I know you're going ask me again to get married. You know I'd love to more than anything, but I've still got that nagging feeling about Thomas". "He can't possibly be still alive, surely you'd have heard something after all these years". Tony stated. "Can we talk about something else ?" Mary asked. "Well I'll never give up, we'll get married one day, even if we're in our nineties". Tony replied slightly frustrated.

Mary returned to the lounge and sank back into the red leather chair, Tony followed bearing a tray of tea and biscuits. "You did very well, that was a lovely meal". Mary said. "I must admit I was a bit worried how it would taste, I made the recipe up myself". "I would write it down for the next time if I was you". Mary replied.

"Try something else Tony, this Midsomer Murders has been on a dozen times". Tony scoured through the channels eventually settling for a couple searching for a property in Devon. "They're looking for sea views for two hundred and eighty thousand, they're hoping". Mary said scornfully. "I couldn't afford to buy my house today, me and Thomas had a bargain at the time". "I haven't got a clue what this old place is worth, I never had to think about buying anywhere, I even inherited a cottage as well, so I suppose I've been very fortunate". Tony added.

"Does anyone ever actually buy a property on these programmes ? I've never seen anyone". Mary said sarcastically.

Tony tuned into an old film staring Robert Mitchum. "This is watchable, it's been on about ten minutes". "This looks like 'River of no return', I saw this years ago at the pictures". Mary recalled.

Gradually their trip down memory lane took away any interest in the film as the subject of conversation again returned to that first meeting on holiday fifty years ago, and had it not been for that old photograph album they would still be non the wiser. “I still find it incredible, just wished it had been me and you together instead of Thomas”. Tony sighed. “We might not be together now if it had been, you probably wouldn't have bothered with me after the holiday. Would you have come knocking like Thomas did ?” “Of course I would”. “I doubt it”. Mary said sadly.

“What do you think of this idea of Robert's, according to Gillian he thinks the strange girl on their wedding photo could be his sister”. Mary said. ”I suppose she could have been in England at the time. The genealogist company might have given her his address”. Mary added. “They'd be in trouble if they had before he'd agreed to meet her”. Tony replied.

“One thing about me staying over at your place, you'll never have any neighbours gossiping”. Mary said as the Mercedes sped along the private drive passing the inquisitive sheep, all grazing within a few inches of the fence. The horses also seemed to be interested, their heads reaching beyond the fence rails to gnaw at the long grassy tufts. “These are my neighbours”. Tony laughed. “And they're only bothered about chewing grass”.

“You can drop me off by the amusement arcade, I want to pop up the High Street”. “I'll park up and wait”. “No, you go on, I'll be a while, I need to get a few bits, it'll save me bothering with the supermarket today”. “Okay then, I'll be round later”..

Mary closed the passenger door and waited on

the footpath as Tony reversed the car to make his return journey. Mary felt pleased that Tony didn't persist as she was looking forward to a stroll along the promenade and a chance to call on Daniel and Debra

****

CHAPTER FOURTEEN

“It's only me”. Tony shouted as he turned the key in the front door. “It had better be, no one else has a key”. Mary shouted back from the kitchen. “Is Robert back home yet ?” Tony asked. “Gillian's on her way to Liskeard now, his train gets in about seven, she rang me the minute she got home from school. She said there was a letter for Robert. She seems to have taken notice of what we said, she said she wasn't going to open it, it's from Italy. She said it feels like there's a photo inside. She sounded almost hysterical with excitement”. “I bet her little fingers are itching to open it, I'm surprised she resisted. Does Robert know ?”. Tony asked. “She said she'd tried him a couple of times, but it went to voice mail, and she really wants to see him when he opens it”

“They'll be here tomorrow, it's football, Robert meets Thomas and they go off in his car, so Gillian said she'd make sure Robert brings the letter for us to read”.

.

A period of silence descended as Tony emptied the grass box for the third time. “I'll have to cut your lawn more often”. One sharp pull on the chord and the noise restarted. “I've had enough, my back's killing me”. Mary shouted into Tony's ear as she walked across the grass to the kitchen door. The lawn mower went quiet again, Tony wheeled the lifeless machine along the paved path and into it's storage position in the garage and emerged carrying a pair of long handled edging shears. “Are you ready for a cup of tea ?” Mary asked through the open window. “I'll be about ten minutes, I'm just going to trim the bottom border then I've finished”

.

The evening was now getting late and Mary was

beginning to wonder if perhaps Gillian would be thinking that it was too late to call. “It doesn't seem as though Gillian's going to ring”. Tony stated. “I ought to be on my way, it's twenty to twelve”.

Mary said goodnight to Tony and as she watched the security lighting darken, and the red rear lights of his Mercedes disappear from view, the telephone rang. Mary grabbed the hall receiver and at the same time kicked the front door shut. “Gillian, are you alright ?” “Yes mum, sorry it's so late, but we've only just got back. Robert came on a later train”. “How is he, I really ought to ask, how's his mum first ?” “His mum's okay, she's on the mend, they've moved her to the general ward this afternoon. That's why Robert was late”. “What about the letter ?”

“Robert trembled when I handed it to him, he was in bits when he read it and saw the photo. She looks lovely, very attractive and slim and ever so stylish, very Italian I suppose”.

“What does the letter say ?” Mary asked impatiently. “She says she can come to England at a moments notice, she's married. I'll bring it tomorrow, you can read it yourself”. “Does she look anything like the girl on the wedding photo ?”

“We've had a quick look on the laptop, it could be her, but I think she would have said something in her letter”. Gillian replied. “How's Robert now, has he settled down ?” “He hasn't been able to keep still, thank goodness he's just gone to bed, he was just beginning to get on my nerves. He can't wait to meet her. I doubt if he'll have much sleep tonight”. “He'll be fine, are you sure he'll want me to see his letter ?” Mary asked. “I think he'd be upset if you weren't interested enough to ask.

I'll let you get off to bed now mum, we'll be over

about one o'clock, see you then, bye". With a huge sigh of relief Mary replaced the handset and went straight upstairs, only to nip back down again to turn off the lights in the lounge.

The clock on the sideboard indicated twenty five past one as Mary stood staring out of her lounge window towards the sea front anxiously waiting to catch sight of Gillian's red Fiesta. "They'll be here soon mum, Robert would never be late for a match". Thomas said. A further ten minutes passed by before Mary hurriedly opened the front door as Gillian's car crunched to a halt on the driveway.

"Sorry we're a bit late mum, it's Robert's fault, he wouldn't come off the computer. He's been trying to find her address on Google Earth, then he's been drafting out a letter to send a reply to her. We've got a basket full of screwed up attempts". "You on about me again ?" Robert called from the pavement while placing his holdall in to the rear of Thomas's car "Just telling mum it's all your fault we're late".

"Hiya Tom". Gillian greeted her eldest brother. "There's no point me coming in, we'll have to dash, you ready Tom". Robert called out as Thomas appeared through the front door.

"Elaine will be here soon, Thomas dropped her off in town". Mary explained. "Well....show me the letter". Gillian carefully took the postcard size photograph from the envelope and discarded the stiff protection card. "So this is Robert's sister, she looks lovely Gillian. She's very good looking, got Robert's hair colour".

Still holding on to the photograph, Mary answered the front door and excitedly ushered Elaine through into the lounge. "Hello Gill, not seen you and Robert for a while, Thomas told me all about his sister". "That's her". Gillian said as Mary handed

Elaine the photograph. "Where did you get this photo ? She's very attractive". "It came with a letter to Robert yesterday". "Could I read it, do you think Robert would mind ?" "Of course you can read it, I've just given it to mum". Mary remained standing and carefully unfolded the sheet of paper and slowly read the neat hand writing.

2 Oct. 2007

Villa Sogno
Via del Tibolsci
San Lorenzo
Roma

Dearest Robert

I'm so pleased and excited to have found you and can't wait to meet you. I was so pleased to hear that you want to meet me. I always knew I had a brother, I was seven when you were born. Our mother unfortunately died in hospital a few weeks later.

I don't know if you ever tried to find our parents. I was born in Rhodesia. Our father sent us to England just before Christmas in 1982. I remember mum telling me it was for our safety. We never saw him again, I've tried for years to find out what happened to him.

After mum died you were taken away and I never saw you again. I was put into care and then into several foster homes.

pto

I do hope you've had a good life. Hope you have had lovely kind parents. Please write back as soon as you've read my letter. Can't wait for your reply Please say where you would like to meet I am ready to fly to England at a moments notice.

I am married to an Italian man, named Gianni Russo. We've been married for thirteen years now.

I enclose a recent photo.

With love, looking forward to seeing you bro'

Jane
xxxx

Having thoroughly read the letter twice, and with a trace of tears trickling down her cheeks, Mary handed the letter to an eagerly awaiting Elaine.

After a few minutes, and also with damp eyes Elaine passed the letter back to Gillian's outstretched hand.

"Has Robert any idea when he will meet her ?" Elaine asked, wiping her eyes with a tissue. "He's drafted out a rough reply, but he can't see his Head letting him have any more school time off. He could make it a weekend but he'd sooner have more time with her, so I think he's going to wait till half term now, it's only two weeks away". Gillian replied.

"He's going to be cheeky and ask the Head anyway before he posts his letter to her". Tears again began to run uncontrollably from Mary's eyes.

"Don't start me off again mum, I've done enough crying with Robert since yesterday". Gillian replied. "While you two are sorting yourselves out I'll put the kettle on for a cup of tea". Elaine joked.

For the following couple of hours, mum, daughter and daughter-in-law past the time by each giving their wisdom as to what Robert ought to do next, where to meet and what to say. "Just listen to us going on with our advice, as if Robert would take a blind bit of notice". Gillian quipped. "Robert already knows what he wants to do". Gillian added.

"That sounds like our men". Elaine pulled open the front door with Tony holding on to his key still inserted in the lock, then feigning a stumble into the hall. "It's not the boys, it's whatshisname". Elaine shouted laughing at Tony's antics. "Who's this whatshisname ?" Tony joked. Elaine and Tony squeezed through the lounge door side by side with linked arms roaring with laughter. "He gets dafter every time I see him". Elaine said cheekily. "Well stop encouraging the silly old fool, he still thinks he's a ladies man.......he wishes". Mary replied

"What's the big secret ?" Tony enquired looking at the wide eyed expression on Gillian's face. "Of course it's Robert's letter, have you got it with you ?" Gillian nodded excitedly and handed it to Tony.

"This must be the lads now". Mary remarked upon hearing the door bell ringing and Elaine again answered the door, Robert and Thomas followed her through to the lounge. "Another three points". Robert bragged. "You've never won again ?" Gillian replied sarcastically. "Four two". Robert added proudly.

Tony returned the letter and the photograph to

Gillian, who promptly passed it on to Thomas. “I think everybody has seen the letter now, what do you think ?” Robert asked. “I don't know about anyone else, but I think she looks wonderful and I want to meet her as much as you do”. Mary answered “We all do”. Elaine added. “I must ring Susan tonight and tell her, she insists I keep her up to date with everything”. Mary said.

“We'll be going now mum, we're going to call on Dan and Debs. Is it okay to tell them Robert ?” Thomas asked. “Course you can, Gillian was going to ring them later on this evening anyway”.

Mary joined the queue in the hallway following behind Thomas, Elaine, Robert and Gillian out to the kerbside, and leaned on the open driver's window to whisper to Thomas. “What did your mum say ?” Elaine asked while pulling at her seat belt. “She thinks Debra may have something to tell us”. “She told me this morning, and asked me not to tell anyone, so act surprised”. Mary muttered. “I think you've just about given the surprise away mum”. Laughed Thomas. “No one should ever trust you with a secret”. “Cheeky devil”. Mary retorted with a smile. Thomas slowly moved away leaving the drive access clear for Gillian to reverse into the road.

Mary resisted the temptation to reveal her news again, and watched and waved as the red Fiesta . went from sight.

Back indoors with only Tony to hear, Mary felt secure to tell her secret. “Tony, I called in on the shop this morning, Debra told me they are going to have a baby. I couldn't say anything before because she'd sworn me to secrecy”. “That was very silly of her”. Tony quipped. “It's about time one of your kids made you a grandmother” “I was beginning to think It would never happen. That's not really fair on our Gillian, she's only just got married" Mary replied. "When is it due ?" "Oh a while yet, she's only just had it confirmed". "I'm surprised you went all afternoon without telling anybody, you're not the best person to trust with a secret. Mind you, you've managed to keep ours safe all these years". Tony muttered with a satisfying smile.

****

CHAPTER FIFTEEN

“I'm surprised you haven't gone to Gatwick with Robert”. Mary said as Gillian swung her legs out of her car scuffing the shingle surface of the drive. “No, I wanted to go but Robert thought it was best he went on his own because Jane was coming alone. If her husband had been coming he would have taken me”. “Did she say how long she intends to stay ?” “She never said, I assume she'll stay while we're on half term. I've got two more days than Robert, his school goes back a week on Tuesday, my new little ones arrive on the Thursday”.

“He's probably getting a bit up tight by now, her plane lands in about half an hour. He was all over the place this morning, couldn't decide what to wear.

Talk about being nervous, he insisted on leaving early, we stood on the platform for nearly an hour waiting for his train”. “He must be getting a bit anxious waiting for her plane to land, I wonder what they'll say to each other when they meet”. Mary said. “He spent half the night keeping me awake because he couldn't get to sleep worrying how they'd get on. Mind you, I couldn't get her out of my head either”. Gillian replied with a sigh.

“How's Robert's mum coping now she's back home ?” Mary asked. “According to his uncle Ron she seems back to her normal self. She was very upset when his uncle told her that Robert had found out about his adoption and got very emotional when she heard he'd got a sister”. Gillian replied. “Does she know today is the big day ?” “Yes, Robert phoned her over a week ago as soon as he knew his uncle had told his mum. He said there was a lot of sobbing, but he said everything was fine and he told her he wasn't annoyed with her. She told him that she had no idea that his birth mother had died or that he had a sister. At the end of the call Robert was in tears as well".

"I don't suppose Thomas will call in this lunchtime, he's no reason to with Robert not playing today, he'll just go straight to the ground. Let's go for a stroll on the beach up to town and we can have some lunch to pass the afternoon away" Mary suggested. "That sounds great, I'll just get my coat from the car". Gillian replied.

"Gillian's only just gone". Mary informed Tony the second he stepped into the hallway. "Has Robert phoned yet ? They must be on their way home by now". "Not yet, Gillian's expecting a call to let her know what time their train gets in". Mary answered. "I'm not expecting to hear from her tonight, she'll most probably be too excited meeting her new sister-in-law".

"That was a nice meal as usual Mary. You go and watch the tele, I'll clear up". "Are you sure you're feeling okay ? This is a first, I won't say no". Taken by surprise Mary dropped onto the settee and reached to the shelf under the coffee table for a batch of magazines.

"The new couple didn't turn up again last Tuesday". Tony shouted, up to his wrists in soapy washing up water. "He did say, what with being a new boy just starting a new job he might not be able to get off every week". Mary shouted back.

Mary continued the high volume conversation. "Me and Gillian had a pub lunch at The Sea Spray, we needed to wrap up a bit walking the beach though". "Was it any good ?" "Not bad, we only had a baked potato and a salad, oh and a shandy each". "It's a nice pub, The Sea Spray, we've not been in there for ages". Tony barked, now almost finished putting away the last of the crockery.

Tony twisted his favourite armchair to square up to the television and promptly pressed his head against the backrest. Mary watched as during the next ten minutes or so he struggled to prevent his eyes from closing, finally falling sound asleep. “Oh well, thanks for the company Tony”. Mary uttered to herself.

The late October Sunday morning was quite chilly with a cold breeze blowing from the coast. Mary shivered as she arrived back to the warmth of her house after her walk to Daniel and Debra's store to purchase her morning newspaper. Immediately she entered the hallway she was alerted by the white light flashing on the answer machine. “You have one new message”. The machine announced in response to Mary pressing the button. “Hello mum, Jane's here, we'll be round this evening to introduce her, about seven, ring me if that's a problem”. Gillian's excited voice echoed out. “End of message”. Concluded the mysterious voice.

Still wearing her winter coat Mary collected the keys to her Mercedes, closed the front door and with one exhaustive heave raised the garage 'up and over' door. Swiftly reversing the car the full length of the drive and onto the road and speeding slightly recklessly for the short distance to the sea front and within a few minutes drawing to a rapid halt back at the corner stores.

“Have you forgotten something Mary ?” Debra laughed as Mary entered. “Gillian's just rung me, they're coming round tonight with Robert's sister to meet me. I need something a bit special”. “ Yes, Gillian rang us this morning to say she'd arrived.

"You'll find a good selection in the chiller cabinet". Debra replied as she followed Mary down the aisle collecting a wire basket on the way. "Do you need any wine ?" Debra enquired. "I'll take a red and a dry white, I've already bought a nice champagne".

Debra lifted Mary's laden basked on to the counter and carefully packed the contents into two plastic carrier bags. "Hope it all goes well tonight, I'm looking forward to meeting her". Debra said as she handed Mary her change. "I'm a bit nervous but I'm sure it'll be fine". Mary replied, and with a bag in each hand returned to her car and the short journey home, driving the Mercedes directly into the already open garage.

Tony duly arrived about an hour earlier than usual as Mary had requested. "You startled me". Mary squealed as Tony quietly entered the kitchen and gently put his arms around Mary's waist. "Come in like yourself next time, you frightened the life out of me". Mary composed herself and returned to preparing more sandwiches.

"Did you get the cakes I wanted ?" Mary asked. "Good job you reminded me, I've left them on the back seat of the car". "It's very cold out there". Tony stated, putting the selection of cakes into the fridge. Mary promptly moved them to a higher shelf, rearranging the day to day items to make room for the platters of sandwiches.

"That's all done, I hope Jane likes fish paste and spam". Mary joked. "Right, I'm going to get changed". "I think you look pretty fantastic in what you're wearing". "Flatterer, and liar". "It's Jane's sister you're meeting, she's not expecting royalty". Tony said with a laugh.

Mary stood at the window looking very attractive, dressed in a slim fitted plain navy blue dress. “For God's sake Mary sit down, they won't get here any quicker”. Tony snapped.

Once again Mary found herself staring out from the lounge window looking across the neighbouring front gardens towards the sea front for the sight of Gillian's red car. For no obvious reason Mary became concerned seeing a string of bunting from one of the private guest houses had come adrift and was flying like a kite, tethered to the swinging B & B sign. “You're making me nervous now with your fidgeting”. Tony chuntered as he crossed the lounge and stood at her side.

“They're here”. Mary squealed as she saw a red Fiesta turn off the promenade. Mary and Tony quickly stepped back from the window as Gillian crunched to a halt on the drive. “Don't seem so anxious, let them ring the bell”. Tony requested. 'Waste of time' he thought to himself as Mary was already standing in the open doorway.

“Mum”. Gillian gasped over excitedly. “Come in quickly out of the cold”. Mary urged. “This is Jane, Jane my mum”. Mary and Jane held and squeezed each others hands for several seconds before kissing each in turn on the cheek. “It's lovely to meet you Jane”. “I'm thrilled to meet you, I've heard so much about you from Gillian”. Jane said returning the greeting. “Do call me Mary. What do you reckon to your sister ?” Mary asked Robert, feeling he was being slightly ignored. “Marvellous”. He replied shyly. Tony stared from the lounge door at the slim pretty young woman dressed equally as stylish as Mary in a smart fitted pale pink coloured two piece suit.

Still holding hands Mary led Jane along the hallway.

“This is Tony, my very good long time friend”.

Tony put his arms around Jane and kissed her cheek. Gillian, standing patiently behind in the hall, whispered to Robert. “Bit more than friends”. “We'll tell you the story about Tony later on Jane”. Mary added. “Let's all get comfortable in the lounge, I hope you haven't eaten. Me and Jane are sitting on the settee”. Mary said leading Jane around the coffee table. “Squeeze up mum it's a three seater” . With Robert and Tony settled comfortably into an armchair each, Mary promptly jumped up. “I'll just put the kettle on for some tea, you give me a hand Gillian”. Within a few minutes Mary returned and covered the coffee table with an orange coloured linen cloth. Gillian laid down a platter of sandwiches, closely followed by Mary with a second platter.

“Who else are you expecting mum ?” Gillian laughed. “Help yourselves”. Mary ordered and began to laboriously describe the contents of each sandwich

“I think some plates would be useful”. Tony remarked with false sarcasm. “I'll go”. Robert was first to react and fetched half a dozen medium sized plates from the kitchen.

Mary and Jane were deep in conversation for several minutes complimenting each other on their choice of outfits until Gillian chipped in excitedly.

“Jane....tell mum about meeting Robert”. Before Jane had chance to speak, Robert, who had been sitting in silence began first. “As soon as I saw Jane's plane had landed I waited for the passengers to come through. I started to panic, I thought I'd missed her, but she was one of the last. We both instantly recognised each other from our photos. I did have a sheet of paper with Jane written on, just in case, but I didn't need it. When Jane smiled coming towards me I started to shake, I was so nervous, but as soon as we held hands we both started crying".

Hearing Robert's voice beginning to quaver with emotion and seeing tears beginning to trickle down his face Jane intervened and continued. "We hugged and after we stopped crying we held hands and had a long chat in the cafeteria with a cup of coffee".

By now Mary and Gillian were finding it difficult to control their emotions and they also began wiping away the tears. "I shouldn't be sniffling, I. already know all this". Gillian said. "We stayed in the cafe for about an hour, then we caught a cab to the station. On the way home Robert told me all about his mum, and his dad. Robert's going to take me to see her later in the week. On the train we told each other our life stories".

"You haven't told us Jane, we know all about Robert, tell us what happened to you". Gillian asked cheekily. "I don't want to bore you with my tales of woe". Jane replied. "You won't, please tell us, I've only heard a few bits". Gillian urged.

Jane began. "I remember our father putting me and mum on a bus to the airport. Mum told me it wasn't safe for us to stay in South Africa and that it was all arranged for us to move to England. This was a week before Christmas in nineteen eighty two . Dad said he'd be with us at Christmas, but he never came, we never saw him again. We went to live in a flat, I can still visualise the place, it was in Horsham.....I remember mum told me.

It might be worth visiting, I can still picture the building and the inside of the flat". "It's not far from where my mum lives, we can go there when we visit mum". Robert interrupted. "Yes, I'd like to do that, I want to see your mum and the flat again". Jane paused to drink the last drop of her tea.

"Me and mum spent Christmas on our own. I remember mum wasn't too surprised dad didn't join us, she said he was never very reliable and he was often missing for several weeks at a time. She did start to get worried but I don't suppose she knew who to contact, I don't think we were in England legally. Then Robert was born in the flat straight after Christmas. I remember mum telling me to knock on the flat next door for some help. I was only seven, I was crying, and one of the neighbours came and looked at mum and ran back to her own flat and called for an ambulance. A lady from another flat came out and looked after me". Jane paused again.

"This must be getting tiresome to listen to ?" "Not at all, it's fascinating, carry on". Mary insisted.

"Anyway to cut it short a bit, mum and the baby were rushed to hospital and I stayed with the neighbour. Then later on in the evening someone collected me and took me somewhere, I can't remember where to, but it wasn't very nice. I remember that much. They took me to see mum a few times but I never saw the baby, Robert, again and then they told me mum had died". Mary saw that Jane was now crying and immediately put her arms around her shoulders to comfort her. Gillian handed Jane a tissue. "I'm sorry". Jane sighed as she wiped away the tears from her eyes.

Mary looked sorrowfully at Jane as she tried to continue. "What was I going to say ?......Oh yes, when they told me about mum I remember I ran out of the building and someone had to chase after me". "You poor girl, didn't anyone take care of you ?" Mary asked. Robert was now in tears, although he had already listened to Jane's life story on the train.

Tony sat in silence, spellbound, occasionally wiping his eyes when he assumed no one would see. "I don't know the name of the home they took me to, but I do remember being taken to my mum's funeral, there was only two other people there. I spent most of my time in foster homes, a couple of them were very nice, but just when I got settled and happy they'd move me to some one else.

My first memory of England when I was seven was landing at Heathrow, I remember dreaming of being an air hostess, after seeing the smart girls on the plane. So as soon as I left school I applied.

I had a letter back listing several vacancies, no hostesses. I finished up with the job they offered me working in the cafeteria". "Did you tell them what to do with it ?" Gillian snapped. "No, I was glad of anything to get me away from the home I was in. It turned out lovely, I'd only been there a couple of weeks when I met Gianni. He was studying law in London, he always stopped for a coffee, and we got chatting, he said I helped him with his English. Then he asked me out, and when I was eighteen we got married in Rome and I've lived there ever since". Mary sighed. "How romantic, what a lovely story".

"Do you speak Italian ?" Gillian enquired. "Yes I can, it took me a couple of years, it was difficult. I went to an evening class but I mainly just picked it up gradually".

"Do you work ?" Gillian asked again". "I don't need to, but I do work as a part time tour guide. I take parties of English and Italian speaking holiday groups around Rome. I'm the lady with the coloured umbrella. At the moment there's not a lot going on so they've said I can have as much leave as I want".

"What does Gianni do ?" Gillian again quizzing. "He's now a lawyer, he works for a large firm in

Rome". Jane replied patiently.

"The name of your villa sounds very grand". Gillian chirped again. "Not really, it's just in a row of typical Italian properties, they all sound fancy in Italian. It was left to Gianni when his mum died about five years ago, she died of bone cancer.

His parents were divorced a long time ago so I never met his father. We've lived there since we were married". Jane concluded with a long sigh of relief. "That's about it".

"I think we should all have a drink now, I've bought a bottle of champagne for this occasion. Will you fetch some glasses Tony ? I have got a couple of bottles of wine if anyone prefers something different. I've bought a dry white and a bottle of red from Debra this morning".

"Jane". Gillian called cheekily, pointing to the unknown lady on a print she'd purposely taken of the particular group photograph. "The sun glare is just covering the lady's face but we thought that it might have been you, she does look a lot like you". Jane joined in the laughter. "I wish I had known in time, then I would be able to say it was me, I would have loved to have been at your wedding".

"I think it's amazing that Robert had only recently found out he was adopted and now he's got a wonderful sister". Tony said sincerely.

"Everyone....to Jane and Robert"..."Jane and Robert". Echoed around the room.

****

CHAPTER SIXTEEN

"That was fascinating last night, what a lovely person for Robert to have as a sister. You could see how much he thinks of Jane". Mary stated. Tony had to wait for a moment to swallow a mouth full of his breakfast before he could speak. "I felt very sorry for Jane, you could see how upset she was getting at telling us about certain things that had happened to her. I'm only surprised she didn't break down sooner than she did". "So am I, her childhood seemed a lot worse than Robert's, at least he had a good mother to take care of him". Mary added.

"You never did get round to telling Jane about how we first met". "I totally forgot all about it after listening to Jane's life story, it went completely out of my head". "I'm surprised Gillian didn't remind us. She's a cheeky young devil, she wouldn't stop, she kept asking Jane all sorts of personal questions" Tony remarked.

"It's as well we both have the same car, the neighbours will assume you didn't bother to put yours in the garage". Tony joked. "They might, as long as they don't remember that mines silver". "Oh well they've seen us together for years now so what's it matter". Tony quipped.

"Beryl next door will probably have a bit of a banter with me over you staying. She's always asking when we're going to get married. I never know whether she's serious, she's always ribbing me. We have a good old laugh together, she's a great neighbour".

"When are we then ?" Tony asked hopefully. "You know the answer to that". Mary snapped. "I don't know if you secretly want Thomas back, what would you do if he did suddenly turn up ?" "I don't know,

I do know I wouldn't want him back as my husband, I'm with you now, so just be satisfied with that". Mary uttered in a mildly angry tone.

"I've got a few things to see to so I'm going to nip off home when I've finished this". Tony said referring to his cooked breakfast. "You watch for the twitching curtains when I drive off". "We're not walking to the pub tonight". Mary ordered. "It's far too cold now, well it is for me anyway". "Right then, I'm off, I'll be back at seven and we'll drive up". Tony said as he left Mary to close the front door.

Tony returned at seven o'clock precisely, Mary met him at the kerbside. ""It is pretty cold tonight". Tony agreed as he drove the Mercedes along the sea front. "I'm going to have a tidy old telephone bill this quarter. I rang Susan this afternoon and we must have talked for over an hour". "How's your mum ?" Tony asked. "Still the same, apparently, Susan says that mum hasn't recognised her once since she went back home".

"Stan and the others are going to be surprised to see us in for a drink tonight, and we're a lot earlier than usual". Tony muttered After a couple of hours of discussion through a wide range of topics, including when Mary and Tony first met, and more interesting the meeting of Robert and Jane.

Although none of the three regulars had ever met Robert, they were all captivated by the story. All they new of Robert was that he had recently married Mary's daughter. "Does his sister have any children ?" One of the two ladies asked. "Not yet, she did say she would like to have children, but she didn't seem to want to talk about it much, so I didn't say any more". "Are you having another Tony ?" Stan asked. "I'd love a beer". Tony said with a smile. "But no thanks Stan, I couldn't face another fruit juice. It's okay for you three, you , live on the door step. We've come in the car tonight". Tony helped Mary with her coat. "We'll see you next Sunday all being well". Tony added

Tony escorted Mary safely in doors. ""I assume we're going to the tea dance tomorrow afternoon, I'll pick you up at two". Mary followed Tony back to the porch, closing the door as his car drove way.

Prompt as ever Tony duly arrived to collect Mary for the Tuesday tea dance, Mary quickly jumped into the car as Tony held open the passenger door. "Good grief, it's a damn sight colder still today than yesterday". Mary said with a shudder and a haunch of her shoulders. "Gillian phoned me this morning, They'd just arrived at Robert's mum's". Mary added. ""I didn't realise they were going today, they never said anything". Tony replied. "Gillian said they only decided on the spur of the moment last night, she's going to give me another call later".

Mary and Tony joined a couple of other regulars and walked across the hotel car park and on into the ballroom. Les thanked Tony for the six pound entrance money that he placed on the table and carried on playing for the several couples dancing to a foxtrot. Tony skirted the edge of the floor to their usual table while Mary stopped to chat for quite some considerable time to several friends, eventually joining Tony just as Les announced the interval waltz.

"Sorry Tony, everyone was asking about Robert and Jane, are you fed up ?" "No, why should I be ? I've had a couple of dances with the twins". "You might think you did, are you sure you danced with both of them ?" Mary joked. "Very funny....I'll fetch the drinks, do you want tea or coffee ?"

"Well.....it wasn't worth going for the dancing

today". Mary said annoyingly, as they travelled along the sea front to the Western end of the promenade, turning right for about a hundred yards and between the brick pillars on to Mary's loose shingle drive.

The warm greeting from the hall radiator was most welcome, Tony hastily closed the door to preserve the heat. Mary tossed her top coat on to the armchair nearest to the lounge door as she entered the kitchen. "I think we only had four dances all afternoon". Mary tutted angrily. "It's a bit early to start dinner, I'll make a pot of tea". She added still with a trace of annoyance in her voice.

Tony stood gazing into the hall mirror combing his wind blown greying hair. "I'm going to the bathroom, I'll drop your coat on the bed". Tony shouted from half way up the stairs. "I don't suppose he'd ever dream of hanging it up". Mary said quietly to herself through gritted teeth. 'He'll be in the bathroom for ages' Mary thought, 'I might as well get the vegetables ready while I'm waiting'.

A good ten minutes later an impatient Mary stood at the foot of the stairs, and in a shrill voice resembling Coronation Street's Hilda Ogden, screeched. "Your tea's on the table going cold". Tony peered over the landing. "I've also done all the vegetables while you've been in there". A clearly irritated Mary shouted. "You've probably just cut the grass and repainted the house as well". Tony muttered under his breath as he descended the staircase. "My god this afternoon's given you the hump". Tony chirped sarcastically. "I hope this mood won't be lasting all night". He added.

Mary jumped up from the table. "That'll be Gillian". She decided as she left the kitchen and picked up the handset in the lounge. "Hello mum"

"Are you back home ?" Mary asked. "No, we've booked into a hotel near Horsham for the night, we ran out of time, we stopped with Robert's mum till after three o'clock, then we went on to find the block of flats were Robert was born".

"How did Jane and his mum get on ?" "Wonderful, that's why we were so long. Robert and his mum were fine as well, it was the first time he'd seen her since his uncle Ron had told her that Robert had found out he'd been adopted, so everything seems to be all sorted out now". "Oh that's good to hear, I'm glad they haven't fallen out. What were the flats like ?"

"Very nice, the whole block has just been refurbished". Gillian paused for a moment to listen to Jane. "I can hear Jane's voice, what's she saying ?" Mary interrupted. "She's asking me to tell you about meeting the lady who helped her mum". "She still lives there then ?" Mary replied.

"It's all very exciting mum. When we found the flats Jane rang the bell to flat eight but no one was in, so she rang number six and a lady answered. She didn't believe who Jane said she was for ages, eventually she asked us up to her flat. She told us a couple of Americans had called on her about a year ago asking questions about Misses Stewart and if she knew what happened to the baby. We assumed they were Jane's Worldwide agents". Gillian paused again to catch her breath.

"She finally really did believe that Jane was telling the truth and actually gave her a big hug. We thought it was fantastic that she was still living there. She said she'd lived in the same flat since the block was built. She told us she could remember Jane's mum and Jane crying outside her door. She said they moved in just before Christmas".

"Did she say much about Jane's mum ?" Mary asked. "She said she remembers speaking to her occasionally but said she wasn't there long enough to get to know properly, she said that Jane's mum seemed to be a very nice lady but she felt that she didn't appear very happy". "What about her dad ?" Mary asked interrupting again. "No she never saw a man there". Gillian replied.

"Robert had an idea, he thought the owners of the flats might still have records. Misses Simpson, that's this lady, gave us the details of the letting agents, she said they'd never changed. So we're going to their offices in the morning, Robert's already phoned and made an appointment. He's hoping they will look into their old records, if they exist. He's hoping he might find some information about his dad, he thinks his dad must have organised the flat lease for his mum. Anyway mum I'll ring you again tomorrow and let you know how we got on. Robert and Jane are saying bye". "Yes I can hear them Gillian, say bye from me".

"My goodness I'm exhausted, that call must have used up all Gillian's credit". Mary informed Tony. "I hope you were listening in on the hall phone, I don't feel like running through all that conversation ". She added. "It all sounds very interesting, I wonder whether they'll get much out of the letting agents, I doubt if they'll be willing to delve back twenty odd years ago". Tony replied.

A pale shaft of early morning sunlight sneaked through a gap in the bedroom curtains casting a tapered strip of light as far as the bed. Mary crossed the floor from her bed and drew back the curtains to reveal the start of another cold day, the watery sunshine attempting to raise the temperature.

"Shopping day". Mary reminded herself out loud. "I could do without that today". She said still talking to herself as she descended the stairs on her way to the kitchen.

"Morning Beryl". Mary shouted across to her neighbour, at the same time struggling to close her garage door. "Morning Mary, it's a bit of a chilly one this morning". Beryl called back as both ladies approached each other either side of the garden wall. After ten minutes of seemingly hilarious conversation and with both ladies beginning to fidget to keep warm, Mary resisted the temptation to extend the discussion. "I must go, I've left my engine running, I'll tell you all about our Gillian's new sister-in-law when I get back". Not having the slightest idea as to what Mary meant, a bemused Mrs. Parker looked on as Mary reversed her silver Mercedes out on to the road and sped away.

Mary was quite surprised to find the supermarket car park unusually extra busy for a Wednesday morning, she thought for a moment that she had her days mixed up. After cruising up and down several lanes she finally located a space.

Inside the store however seemed relatively normal. Mary made her customary dash around the shelves, knowing exactly what she wanted and where to find it, returning after about twenty minutes with her laden trolley to the checkout with the shortest queue.

Mary carried her heavy shopping carrier bags one in each hand dropping them on the floor just inside the hallway, then repeating the journey a further three times. With all her groceries safely indoors she began the laborious task of storing all the items in the fridge and the various cupboards when the door bell rang.

"Who the hell's that". She muttered quietly as she stepped over and around the bags to reach the door. “Oh....it's you Beryl, come on in, mind the shopping bags, go on into the kitchen, you'll have to excuse me for a few minutes while I sort out my frozen stuff”. Mary shuffled back and forth. “I think that's everything for the fridge”.

Mary quickly took off her coat and filled the kettle. “Tea or coffee Beryl ?” Mary asked. “Coffee please, I'm sorry, I should have waited an hour or so before I came round, but you know me, I was curious when you said about Gillian's new sister”. “Sister-in-law”. Mary corrected. “Oh, I was wondering how she could suddenly have a sister”.

Beryl listened intently as Mary began to tell the whole story of Robert discovering that he'd been adopted and the fascinating events about the sister he never knew existed The sound of the door bell ringing again interrupted Mary.

Mary stood bewildered in the open doorway, surprised to be confronted by two uniformed female police officers. “Misses Hooper ?” The elder and more senior of the two officers presumed. “Yes, that's right”. Mary replied hesitantly. “Can we come in for a moment ?” The oldest officer asked.

“I'll be out of your way Mary, see you later”. Beryl said as she squeezed past in the hallway, not wanting to intrude. Mary was now too concerned to take any notice when the police officers produced their identifications. “Is Gillian Hooper related to yourself ?” The senior lady officer asked politely. “She's my daughter”. Mary answered with her obvious anxiety drying up her mouth. “Has something happened to her ?” “We've been contacted by the Reigate constabulary that she has been involved in a motor accident”. The younger of the two officers immediately put an arm around Mary. “Don't worry, I know what you're thinking, she is in hospital, but her injuries aren't life threatening", This attempted assurance did not reduce Mary's condition. "Are you sure she's going to be alright ?" Mary begged. "She hasn't anything life threatening, that's all we've been told" "What about her husband and his sister ?"

"We understand that she was alone in the car" "I don't understand, they were altogether, how do you know it's my daughter ?" Mary cried. "Apparently there was a driving licence in the glove compartment with this address". The oldest of the two officers replied. "Yes, she passed her test when she was single and living at home. But I still don't know why she was driving on her own". Mary repeated.

"Do you have phone numbers for them ?" One of the officers enquired. At this stage Mary's heart beat had almost returned to a near normal pace. She collected the address book from the hall table and handed it to the younger officer indicating Robert's number. "That's Gillian's number, but I don't have one for Jane, Robert's sister". Mary added. "Would you like us to try and contact Robert for you ?" "If you would please, I'll be okay in a minute, I'll probably want to speak to him". Mary thought for a moment or two. "I think I ought to phone him myself".

"Hello Robert". "It's Jane, is that you Mary ?" "Yes. Where's Robert ?" "He's just gone back to the letting agent's car park, Gillian drove off on her own. he's gone to see if she's back there. Oh, he's just crossing the road ". "Don't panic, she's been in a car accident". "Oh God". Jane squealed. Robert snatched the phone from Jane's hand. "Who's this ? Oh it's you Mary, what's the matter ?" "I was just telling Jane, Gillian has had an accident, she's okay, don't worry". "How do you know ? What happened ?" Robert asked anxiously. "The police told me... .they're still here with me. Why was she on her own, what's going on ?" "We had a bit of an upset in the agents office and she left the office. When me and Jane got outside the car had gone. We've just been waiting around for the past couple of hours for her to come back. Are you telling me the truth, she isn't badly hurt ?" "That's what the police have told me". Mary answered. "Which hospital is she in ?" "Do you know which hospital she's in ?" Mary asked the lady officers. After a short pause. "You need to ring the police at Reigate, have you got a pen and paper ". Mary proceeded to read the number being displayed by the police officer. "Why did they call on you ?" Robert asked. "Gillian's driving licence was in the glove compartment". Mary replied.

Jane regained possession of Robert's mobile telephone. "Robert's getting a bit upset Mary, She is alright, isn't she ?" Jane asked impatiently. "I can only tell you what the police have told me. What caused Gillian to drive off on her own ?" Mary asked again. "She and Robert had quite an upset in the letting agents". "What about ?" "Robert will tell you when we get back. I'm going to ring that police number now Mary. I'll ring you as soon as we know where she is. Was anyone else hurt ?" Mary mouthed the question to the senior lady officer. "Apparently there wasn't any other vehicle involved". "I'll ring you later then Mary, bye", Jane disconnected the call and immediately pressed in the number Mary had read out.

The two officers accepted Mary's offer of a cup of tea and chatted until the telephone rang. This was the first chance Mary had to relax and observe the young attractive uniformed police ladies.

"Mary....she's actually been brought here to Crawley, we don't know where the hospital is so Robert's popped back into the letting agents offices to ask them for the number of a taxi firm". Jane said hurriedly. "Ring me from the hospital as soon as you've seen her". Mary requested. "Course we will, have to go now, Robert's just coming back and this could be our taxi, that's quick". Before Jane could ring off. "What caused Gillian to go off on her own in the first place ?" Mary asked again. "I've got to go Mary, it is our taxi, Robert will see you when we get back".

The two lady police officers both shook hands with Mary as they departed, leaving her alone anxiously awaiting news from the hospital. Mary watched from the lounge window as the police car drove away, then hastily stepped back from view and peered from behind the curtain as Beryl and her husband drove on to their drive, hoping she hadn't attracted Beryl's attention.

Mary nervously wandered from room to room keeping an eye on the time as the hands on the clock rotated....three, four, five, six o'clock came and still no call. Still standing staring at the time with the telephone handset firmly gripped in her right hand willing it to ring. Mary decided in her mind that she would wait until seven o'clock, then she would contact the hospital herself.

"I hope Beryl doesn't suddenly decide to come back round". Mary sighed out loud, wondering what the other neighbours would be imagining having seen the police vehicle outside her house for over an hour.

The piercing ring of the telephone startled Mary, causing her to temporarily fumble locating the receive button. "Sorry we've took so long to call Mary, we've only just been able to see her". "I was getting worried Jane, how is she ?" Mary nervously asked, her voice stuttering with fear. "She's in the intensive care unit, she'll be there for a few days. They suspect she may have some broken ribs, she's having an x-ray at the moment. We're just waiting for her to come back". "Has Gillian said anything ?" "Not yet, we only saw her for a few minutes before they took her to the x-ray room.

She was in tears when she saw Robert". Jane said sorrowfully. "Is Robert alright ?" "Mary asked. "Yes he's just wandered off to find a coffee. "What happened in the letting agents ?" "Robert will see you tomorrow sometime, he'll tell you. I can't say really, it might not be true". Jane replied hesitantly. "Oh come on Jane, something made Gillian go off on her own". Mary persisted. "Honestly Mary, I would sooner you let Robert tell you. He will see you tomorrow, we've booked in the hotel for tonight and we'll catch the train after we've seen Gillian. If you hang on she's just come back from x-ray".

Immediately Gillian's bed was back in it's position a gentleman in a smart grey suit arrived. "Is the lady's husband here ?" He asked as Robert entered the intensive care unit. "Yes I'm here".

The two men shook hands, and Robert introduce his sister Jane. Mean while Mary had the handset pressed hard against her right ear unsuccessfully trying to hear the background chatter. Mary hung on patiently for some ten minutes before Jane eventually continued the conversation.

"Are you still there Mary ?, The doctor's with her now, he says she has two or three broken ribs and they're concerned that one in particular might puncture her lungs. He says they can't do anything tonight and she'll be operated on first thing tomorrow morning. He said not to worry too much, the surgery is more exploratory, just to be on the safe side".

"She must be in a lot of pain". Mary stated. " It's mainly breathing that hurts, she's got some nasty bruises on her face and her top half, but the sister said they'll fade in a few days. Anyway we'll be coming back tomorrow, Robert said it'll probably be Saturday when we come round. He said we'll stay here with Gillian as late as we can. We'll give you a call when we're on the train".

Mary replaced the telephone onto it's base and. was now sat in total darkness, gazing through the lounge window at a faulty street lamp flickering on the opposite side of the road.

It was precisely this time of the day that Tony would arrive, this evening she was wishing he wasn't coming as she didn't particularly feel like company. However as punctual as ever she heard a key being inserted into the front door. "What's for dinner ?" Tony joked as he closed the door. "Good God Mary, it's freezing in here, has your heating packed up ?" "I forgot to switch it back on after lunch. I've had a terrible day, I never noticed how cold it's got". "Let's get some lights on, what are you doing sat in the dark ?" Tony asked as he reset the boiler. "Come on....tell me, what's up ?" Tony became quite distressed as Mary unravelled the days events.

"Has no one said how the accident happened ?" Tony asked earnestly. "Not yet, I daresay we will hear from the police sometime tomorrow, they should know something by then, they must have taken the car away by now". Mary assumed. "Jane's going to ring after Gillian's had her operation tomorrow.

They're staying as long as they can then catching the train home". "Why don't we drive up there early in the morning, we can see Gillian and then bring Robert and Jane home". Tony suggested. "That would be a great relief to see her. Are you sure you want to drive all that way ?" "You know my feelings for Gillian, you'd better ring Robert straight away, we'll need to get going about six. Tell

Robert we'll come straight to the hospital, we should be there for elevenish". Jane again answered the call on Robert's telephone. "Get the name of the hospital". Tony whispered in Mary's free ear. "I'll just nip out and fill the car, save wasting time in the morning, won't be long".

Tony reversed the refuelled Mercedes out onto the road then travelled the short distance to the seafront and along the promenade. The chilly but dry early November morning felt even cooler inside the car for the first mile due to the air conditioning working at full blast. Tony took advantage of the lack of early morning traffic and soon left Plymouth behind and now speeding on towards Exeter. "I think we can do without the satnav for a while". Tony remarked at the same time tapping the mute button to silence the irritating interruptions.

Mary woke up as Tony located a place in the hospital car park and switched off the engine. He positioned his seat as far back as it would travel, "What time is it ?" Mary asked with a stifled yawn.. "Ten past eleven". Tony replied while stretching his legs under the bulkhead. "Which way to the hospital entrance ?" Mary asked desperately needing to visit the toilets.

Once inside the main entrance Mary and Tony disappeared to their respective toilets. When Mary returned Tony was already at the reception desk making enquiries.

With a hospital layout in hand they entered the nearest available lift to the required floor level and after a hesitant wander along the corridor, leaving an unsure Mary several yards behind. Tony softly called out. "Come on, this is it, it's here".

Tony pressed the white plastic push button

mounted on the wall to the side of the double width doors. “Hello, can I help you ?” “Yes please, we're here to see Gillian Hines, she was admitted yesterday. It's her mother and a friend”.

“Push the door and come on through”. A nurse's voice instructed. Robert came part way along the short corridor to intercept Mary and Tony and without saying a word they followed him to Gillian's bedside.

Jane promptly jumped up from her chair adjacent the bed and gave Mary a hug and a kiss on the cheek. Mary gazed sympathetically at Gillian and was a bit shocked to see the extent of bruising to her eyes and her face.

“She's not long come back from the operating theatre, the sister has only just brought her round”. Jane said. “She looks very tired, how do you feel Gillian ?” Mary asked. Gillian attempted to smile but she remained silent. “I think she's hurting too much to talk”. The ward sister stated as she approached to check on Gillian. “The doctor will be along shortly to have a chat with you”.

Mary sat in the other seat by the bed. Looking at the sad expression on her daughter's bruised face, she was forced to discreetly wipe away her tears.

Tony stood chatting quietly to Robert while shifting his weight from leg to leg in a rocking motion. “Robert's just telling me, the police called round this morning but they weren't allowed to see Gillian yet. They said a witness statement from a motorist following, said she just went off the road into a drainage ditch, as if she'd fainted or fallen asleep at the wheel. They've given Robert the name and address of the garage that collected the car”.

“The doctor's just with the next bed at the moment, he won't be a minute”. The ward sister announced as she returned to be present. “Those bruises will disappear soon". She advised, obviously seeing Mary's worried expression. "She'll be in some discomfort in turning over and breathing with those broken ribs, they should heal in about eight to ten weeks". She added.

"Did they have a row ?" Mary whispered to Jane across the bed. "No, it's nothing like that. Robert will tell you later". Jane replied, hoping Mary would not keep asking her.

"We're only supposed to allow two visitors at a time, but as you've come such a long way it'll be okay". The sister explained pleasantly as a very smart suited gentleman suddenly appeared in the bed space. "Good afternoon everyone....I'm Phillip Leeson". Mary and Jane instinctively began to rise from their chairs beside the bed. "You're fine, please stay seated, I assume you're Gillian's mother ?" "Yes, this is her husband and her sister-in-law, and this is my very good friend.". Mary answered,

"Well Gillian, you're a very lucky young lady". Gillian tried to smile but her need to close her eyes and go back to sleep gave the impression that she wasn't listening. However the surgeon continued to explain. "We had to operate because we were afraid that one of your ribs could have punctured your lung. You'll be in a fair amount of pain for a while. Try not to take any sudden deep breaths. We'll do our best to make the pain bearable". Gillian opened her eyes and mouthed a silent. "Thank you". "Oh, by the way, your baby's fine and healthy". Phillip Leeson calmly said. This news appeared to upset Gillian and tears began to run across her battered face damping the pillow.

Mary gasped. "Do you already know ?" She asked excitedly staring at Robert and then at Jane.

"Have a safe journey home I understand you've come up from Cornwall. Don't worry too much about

Gillian, she's in safe hands". The suited Mr. Leeson interrupted as he moved on to his next patient.

"How long have you known ?" Mary asked Jane. "I only found out yesterday, Robert told me while we were waiting for Gillian to come back". Jane answered. Robert stood at the end of the bed gazing at Gillian who had now succumbed to her heavy eyes and fallen asleep.

"You've not said a lot Robert, when did you know ?" Mary asked repeating the question. Robert quickly wiped his eyes with a tissue. "We only knew a couple of weeks ago". He said sharply. Mary felt that Robert didn't seem very interested at the prospect of Gillian having a baby and she put his abnormal abruptness down to his worries for Gillian.

The ward sister a slightly plump lady, probably in her late forties, returned from her round visit of the ward. "Gillian will stay here for a couple more days, then all being well we'll move her to a general ward and as soon as we control her pain she'll be able to go home". "How long do you think that will be ?" Mary politely enquired. "She should be back home by this time next week". The sister replied.

"Well Gillian isn't going to need us for a while, she's fast asleep. I think we ought to make tracks". Tony suggested. Mary raised herself from her chair, gently squeezing her daughter's hand and kissed her on her forehead, at the same time noticing that Gillian was crying in her sleep . Tony followed Mary and held Gillian's hand for a tender moment. "Did you notice the tears trickling down her face ?" Mary whispered to Tony. "Yes, it must be because of the pain she's in, she's certainly fast asleep".

Leaving the ward they each thanked the nursing staff. The solid looking oak security doors closed slowly with the group lost for a moment in a wide empty corridor. "It's this way". Tony decided.

"We'll have to just pop back to our hotel, they let us leave all our things with reception". Jane added .

The long laborious drive home was mainly in silence. Mary from time to time attempted to engage Robert in conversation, hoping he would reveal what had happened at the letting agents. Tony refuelled his Mercedes whilst Mary and Jane quickly collected an assortment of pre-packed sandwiches from the mini one stop store.

Tony eventually gave in to Mary for persistently insisting to share the driving. "I am capable". She taunted. "My car's exactly the same, I do know how to drive". Although he wouldn't admit it, Tony was secretly pleased to swap seats with Mary and relax for the remaining hundred or so miles.

Mary was relieved to be able to slump onto her settee after a long arduous day, having made a detour to Robert's cottage. Tony joined Mary on the settee bearing two mugs of hot chocolate,

"What a day, you do realise we will have to do that trip again next week sometime to fetch Gillian". Tony said. "As long as she's going to be alright I don't mind. I still think there's something wrong, what reason did Gillian have to go dashing off in the car like that ?" Mary asked.

"Who'd have thought it......a week ago I was convinced I'd never be a grandmother, now I'm going to have two beautiful grandchildren next year".

****

CHAPTER SEVENTEEN

"Is Gillian any happier ? She's been home nearly a fortnight now". Tony asked. "She did phone me yesterday, she told me the district nurse has seen her every day since she came home. She still sounds upset about something. She wouldn't tell me anything either". Mary replied. "It's good they're keeping an eye on her". Tony stressed. "She's still worrying the life out of me". Mary said fretfully.

"Robert's off to Reigate this morning to collect Gillian's car, a neighbour took him to the station". Mary informed.

"Do you want to pop over and keep Gillian company for a couple of hours ?" Tony asked. "It's a pity Jane had to go home". He added. "She's coming back in two weeks time with her husband to stay for Christmas. Yes...I'd love to spend the afternoon with Gillian, perhaps she'll tell me what's going on with her and Robert. Neither of them have been near since we fetched her out of hospital. I've spoken to Gillian on the phone a few times. I only found out that Robert was going for the car through Thomas". Mary sighed sorrowfully. "I can't understand it, what's gone wrong, they were both so excited at meeting Jane. Since they went up to see the flat at Horsham everything seems to have changed". Mary added. "Well, let's see if Gillian feels well enough and ask her and Robert over for dinner tomorrow night. Let's see if we can't get to the bottom of it once and for all". Tony replied forcefully.

Mary could see that Gillian was still in a great deal of pain as she opened the cottage door. "Oh, hello mum...Tony, I wasn't expecting you". "We thought you might like some company for a couple of hours. Have you been crying again ?" Mary asked sympathetically. Gillian ignored the question and gingerly walked back and carefully sat in her armchair. "Have you made yourself any lunch ?" Mary asked. Gillian shook her head. "Tony, go and make a sandwich". Mary instructed, and sat down in the chair facing Gillian. "You're coming over to me tomorrow for dinner". Mary ordered.

"Has Robert phoned to say what time he'll be back with your car ?" "He phoned an hour ago, he'd stopped near Winchester for a bite to eat, reckons he'll be home by seven". Gillian answered in a strained voice. "Isn't your pain getting any easier ?" Mary enquired seeing how Gillian winces and holds her chest with each breath. "It's not too bad, it's getting better, still painful to take a deep breath. Turning in bed's the worse.

I've got a hospital appointment on Monday, to save Robert having to take any more time off work, will you take me ?" "Of course, but you and Robert will, I mean it, you will come tomorrow, I want to know what's still upsetting the pair of you". Gillian looked sheepishly away from Mary's gaze.

"Here you are Gillian, it's only cheese and tomato, I couldn't find anything else". Tony said as he placed the plate on Gillian's lap. "I've made a pot of tea, just letting it stand a bit". "Robert and Gillian are coming tomorrow". Mary informed Tony at the same time aiming an instructive glare at Gillian.

Robert supported Gillian as she struggled to get out of the passenger seat of her red Fiesta. Mary met them on the drive and held Gillian by the arm as they entered the house. Tony waited in the hall and carefully helped Gillian to remove her coat and led her through to a comfortable armchair in the lounge. Robert sat in the opposite chair nervously clutching some folded papers.

"I've just been and had a look at your car. I can't say I can tell where the damage was, it looks brand new". Tony commented. "It was mainly the bonnet and the nearside front wing, I think they made a good job of it". Robert replied.

Mary appeared from the kitchen with the customary tray of teas and when she had handed each a drink, sat down besides Tony on the settee.

"Right then you two, no more avoiding the issue, I know there's something wrong. Why did you drive off on your own....what's been going on ?" Mary demanded.

"You're not going to be very pleased mum". "Go on, lets hear it". Mary interrupted.

"Me and Robert are brother and sister, we've got the same father". Gillian blurted out and immediately burst into uncontrollable sobbing. Mary and Tony looked at each other in amazement. "Don't be stupid Gillian, where's this come from ?" Mary replied angrily.

Robert stood from his chair and handed Mary the papers he had been nursing. "These are photo copies the letting agents gave us. The lady at the agents had these details for us as soon as we got to their office. She has two brothers living in that block of flats so she said she was interested to search for us". "Well what are these papers supposed to tell me ?" Mary asked. "Read them mum, or listen to Robert". Gillian snapped.

"I assumed our dad, thinking of me and Jane, arranged the lease of the flat for mum, and we might find the name and address of a witness, normally it's someone he'd know". By now Tony and Mary were engrossed in the documents. "This says the lease is in the name of K.J.Stewart". Tony muttered. “Yes but this other document was attached to the original lease and you can see the deposit was paid by cheque and the six month rent by cash. And if you look there, the receipt is made out to Thomas Hooper”.

Mary and Tony were stunned into silence, Mary could feel her blood pressure rising and her face feeling hot and flushed. “It's obviously some other Thomas Hooper”. She urged. “Maybe it is, but why is our father's name down as Barnes on mine and Jane's birth certificates ?” By now Gillian had stopped crying and rejoined the discussion. “We are going to get a separation mum, and I've had a word at the hospital about a termination, but they've told me to wait until I'm better. I'm sorry but there's no other way”.

“Rubbish”. Mary shouted scornfully at Gillian. Tony stared at Mary in anticipation of her next words.

“Your father isn't Thomas Hooper anyway, your real father is sitting on this settee with me. It's Tony. So now you know”. Mary had now convinced herself and was extremely angry with thoughts of her husband's double life all those years ago, although she felt a pang of hypocrisy for having an affair with Tony.

“I don't believe you mum, why didn't you ever tell me ? I would have loved Tony to be my dad” “Well I never expected my husband to disappear and I never wanted to spoil the relationship you have with Thomas and Daniel”.

Mary gave Tony a sharp kick on his shin. “You say something”. She urged. Gillian again began to cry and Tony couldn't prevent his eyes welling up and tears trickling down his cheeks.

For the past twenty odd years Tony had yearned for the moment he could reveal that he was Gillian's father, but wished it could have been under different circumstances.

"It all fits". Robert said suddenly, and added "My mother lived in South Africa, Jane was born there and Thomas Hooper worked there all through the seventies . It must be the same person". Mary couldn't see any other conclusion and reluctantly accepted that the long months that Thomas was away were spent using a false identity and another life, and a new family.

"I think you're just saying that Tony is my dad to keep us together, we've already seen a solicitor for his advice, we've got another meeting with him next week". "Well for God's sake cancel it, don't you think that if I thought there was any chance of you and Robert being brother and sister that I would want it to continue ? Of course I wouldn't. Tony is your father". Mary emphasized. "So for goodness sake get this divorce and abortion idea out of your heads. You do believe me now, don't you ?"

Gillian finally stopped crying and for the first time since her motor accident a smile appeared on her face as she squeezed in between Mary and Tony on the settee and held his hand. No one spoke for a while but at this moment Tony knew he now had his daughter and that everything was going to be alright.

Gillian broke the silence. "I understand now why you've been so generous to me. The cottage, and lots of gifts, and that cabin upgrade". "Well you are my daughter". Tony answered. "Thank you dad". Gillian said, putting a tearful smile on Tony's face.

"You do understand now Gillian ? I'm your mother and Tony is your father........Robert's mother was Katherine Stewart and his father was Thomas Hooper. So there's no blood line between you and Robert at all".

Robert rose from his chair and took Gillian's hand

and together they went into the dining room to be alone for a while.

Meantime Mary was busy scribbling her version of their family tree on a scrap sheet of paper. “Clever devil”. Tony chirped. “Show Gillian when they come back”. The obvious detail her tree revealed was that Mary's sons , Thomas and Daniel where now Gillian's half brothers. Mary hoped Gillian had already realised this for herself and wouldn't get upset..

Gillian entered the lounge and sat on the arm of the settee. “That looks complicated, so Tony's....I mean dad's parents were my grandparents. I did meet them once when I was ten or eleven”. Tony smiled to himself that Gillian had accepted him immediately and was already referring to him as 'dad'.

“Robert”. Mary shouted to her son-in-law as he was pouring himself a glass of lemonade in the kitchen. “I've just thought of something. Thomas always kept all his overseas expenses records and bank statements and empty cheque book stubs. I remember years ago Daniel dumped them all in the loft for me. I've no idea what's there, I never had anything to do with his private expenses, they're in one of those big clear plastic boxes. If you want to have a look be careful up there, it could be anywhere”.

“I'll just put the pasta on to boil, the casserole must be ready by now, Gillian will you lay the table ?” Mary asked. Tony moved over to his favourite armchair and relaxed with a smile of contentment on his face.

“Dinner”. Mary called out, it's on the table. “Robert's not still in the loft ?” Mary quipped. “Pop up stairs and give him a shout, he'll need a bath by the time he gets down”. Mary added. “Dinners ready Robert, have you found it ?" Tony shouted at the hole in the ceiling. "No...there's so much junk up here". Robert's voice echoed. "You're covered in cobwebs". Tony said as Robert descended the loft ladder. "I'll have another look after dinner".

"Robert's on his way, he's just in the bathroom getting rid of the cobwebs". Tony informed as he took his seat at the dining table. "Has he found it ?" Mary asked.

"I'll have another go later". Robert answered from the hallway just as he entered the dining room. "I've left the ladder down". "It's a casserole, I know you all like beef". Mary said. "Careful, the plates are very hot". She added.

"He won't give up, he's back in the bloomin' attic". Tony chuntered. "Oh...leave him up there, go and shut the lid". Gillian joked. "You're full of the joys of spring now Gillian". Mary suggested. "At the moment mum, I've no pains, I'm not hurting anywhere, everything is perfect. I've got my dad, and you of course". Gillian said with a satisfactory sigh. "You've made him cry again, big softy". Mary said glancing at a tearful Tony.

Tony stood on the third tread of the ladder as Robert lowered a dusty plastic box to within his reach. "Is this what you've been looking for ?" "I hope so, it was buried under some old carpets and rolls of wallpaper. Why Mary kept all this junk I don't know". Robert moaned.

For the second time inside an hour Robert had to clean himself up. "You've found it then Robert ?" Mary confirmed. "Is it okay if I take it home to look through ? It's late now and it'll probably take ages. We need to be going. You ready Gill ?" Robert asked. "I'd be interested to know what you find , ring me". Mary urged.

****

CHAPTER EIGHTEEN

Gillian stood at Mary's side with Thomas as Tony's best man on this chilly Saint Valentine's morning as the Registrar pronounced Tony and Mary, 'husband and wife'. Seated in the small Registry Office, the immediate family including Jane and her handsome Italian husband, Gianni, and a few close friends gave a rapturous round of applause as the lady Registrar made the announcement. The early morning wedding was followed by a modest 'brunch' style reception meal a few minutes walk away at the Knoll House Hotel.

"Speech....speech". "That must be Susan". Tony quipped as he obediently stood to attention, receiving a pat on the shoulder from Mary.

"I haven't made any notes, so I won't be boring you for long. I'd just like to say that this Christmas just gone has given me the best Christmas presents I've ever had, or could ever have wished for. I've got my daughter, Gillian, and a complete family who've always treated me as a family member for the past twenty six years. And at long last on Christmas Day Mary finally accepted my engagement ring. And to top it all I'm going to be a granddad.

Lastly, I'd just like to thank my new sister-in-law, Susan for bringing back those forgotten memories of fifty years ago". Susan shouted back in response. "It's just a pity it wasn't you who came knocking on Mary's door. Never mind, you got the right girl in the end". "That's true, I think every one's heard the story and knows what Susan's talking about". Tony replied. "Also, thank you to Thomas for being my best man and my Gillian for giving her mother to me, and thanks to all of you for coming, and your presents".

Tony half sat down then sprung back up. “Sorry, I forgot to say Mary and me will be leaving in about ten minutes. Somewhere we need to be”, “I can guess where that is”. Susan Interrupted. “I'm sure you can, Susan. Anyway just to say, the room's booked till three o'clock and the bar bill's paid. So enjoy the music and the afternoon dancing”. Tony received an appreciative chorus of applause as he sat back down.

Stepping out into the cold February air, Tony and Mary followed by their guests all laughing as Thomas drove Tony's Mercedes up to the front of the main hotel entrance. “Look at the state of that”. Tony exclaimed. “That's Susan and Gillian for you, I'll bet”. Apart from the wedding ribbons and the sophisticated set of silver bells in the rear windscreen, there was an array of tin cans and silly balloons attached somehow from inside the boot lid.

“We'll soon get rid of that when we get round the first corner”. Tony said laughing. “I hope no one's messed with our suitcases......Susan ?” “I wouldn't dream of it Tony, have a lovely cruise”.

“You have got the passports in you bag ?” Tony asked. Mary smiled and waved as she sent her seat back to it's maximum position.

“Why have we had to dash off so early ? Where are we staying tonight ? How come Susan thinks she knows ?” Mary asked as the Mercedes descended the steep hill overlooking Chesil Beach as they approached the village of Abbotsbury. Tony chose to ignore Mary's salvo of questions and carried on singing to himself to a Matt Monroe CD. A few minutes later Tony observed that Mary's chin was resting on her chest, and that she'd fallen fast asleep. 'Must be my singing, it usually does that'. Tony thought as Mary's head fell on his shoulder.

"Where are we ?........Corfe Castle" Mary gasped as she opened her eyes. "There's the castle". Mary shouted, pointing to the majestic ruined structure as they stopped at the traffic lights after negotiating the winding hill between the Purbeck stone cottages. "I remember this place, we came here from.....You're going to Swanage". Mary screamed as she at last realised. "You romantic old softie you". "I can't believe you hadn't guessed when Susan gave it away. Anyway I've booked a night in a nice hotel, and I didn't want to get there too late. We've got plenty time to get to Southampton tomorrow".

The car reached the sea front and turned right and travelled along the promenade and slowly drew to a halt opposite the amusement arcade. The drab February skies didn't deter their spirits, Tony did a silly dance step as he skipped back from purchasing a parking ticket while Mary grappled with her warm overcoat. "This is why I wanted to get here early, let's wander over and go on the pier before it closes". Tony suggested. "This building wasn't here in nineteen fifty eight". Mary noted referring to the theatre as they strolled along the sea front beneath the overhanging canopy.

"We're the only two people on the pier". Mary observed. "No one else would be this daft on a freezing cold afternoon". Tony quipped as they set off along the boarded deck towards the end of the pier and up the short flight of steps.

"Remember this ?....this is where we first met". "Yes, I remember it well". Mary replied softly as they leaned on the ornamental railing looking back at the sweep of the shoreline illuminated by the street lamps along the length of the promenade. At their feet they tried with the help of the torch light on Tony's mobile telephone to read the messages engraved on the brass plaques rebated into the ends of every floor plank.

"Are you sure we should be on here ?" Mary asked. "Well I paid, the fella knows we're on here so I hope he lets us off before he locks up". Tony replied. "You do realise nowhere will be open this time of the year, I assume we're eating in the hotel, I'm starving now". Mary moaned. "I intended it to be a surprise...there's a Valentine's dinner dance tonight at the hotel, eight till midnight". "Oh that's lovely, I'm looking forward to that". Tony could feel Mary shivering with the cold as they looked across the bay towards the feint outline of 'Old Harry Rocks' just visible in the fading light.

The sound of the water below, lapping against the pier structure provided a musical backdrop for Tony as he began to sing in a deep but surprisingly melodious voice. **"some encharrn..ted evening...you may see a straingerrr you may see a........"** As he carried on singing in a serious attempt to keep a straight face. Mary though to herself. 'Is this a romantic coincidence or does he know something'. Then catching sight of the stupid grin on his face, Mary burst out laughing. "You daft bugger".

****

CHAPTER NINETEEN

Looking back at the docked cruise liner on which they had just spent the past twenty one days, already being prepared for it's evening departure, Tony and Mary slowly made their way from the dockside to the waiting vehicle to return them to the car storage compound.

"Well it's still here, looks in need of a clean". Tony commented, spotting his pale blue Mercedes tightly hemmed in a parking space from both sides. "I'll reverse out a bit, you'll never open your door".

"What's the matter ?" Mary enquired as she stood shivering from the cold with two large suitcases at her side. "Damn thing won't start, battery's flat". "Click....click". As Tony again turned the key in the ignition. "I guessed as much when I needed the key to open the door". "What do we do now then ?" Mary asked. "I'll have to pop back to the office, see if they've got someone who can help. Sit inside the car while I go and see, my sides the easiest, it's a bit of a squeeze". About twenty minutes later Tony returned, shortly followed by a white transit van.

Within minutes the van driver produced a set of leads and very soon the Mercedes burst into life. After Tony had thanked the young man with a palmed five pound note, Mary reversed the car into the open, got out of the vehicle and into the passenger seat. Tony tapped away at the satnav keyboard for a couple of minutes before driving out of the compound....."Now turn left". Interrupted the faceless voice.....and into the busy midday traffic.

Turning off the sea front after a traffic laden four hour journey, Mary's house, their future joint home, and Gillian's red car at the kerbside was a welcome sight. Tony gave a sigh of relief as he switched off the engine and stepped out and stretched his legs in the freezing March air.

“How long have you been waiting ?” Mary called out to Gillian as they approached the open front door. “I've been here a couple of hours, get inside out of the cold. Debra popped in early this morning and put your heating on. I'll make a pot of tea”. “We could do with something, I'm starving, we never bothered to stop”. Tony said at the same time bending to switch on the electric fire. “Are you that cold dad ?” Gillian asked. “It's the change from all that hot sunshine over the last three weeks”. “It looks as though it did you some good, you're both lovely and brown”. “You should have seen him a week ago, he looked like a cooked lobster”. Mary joked. “But we did have a fantastic holiday, you know yourself what your cruise was like”. Mary added.

“Anyway, something to tell you. I know you still think that Robert's dad Thomas Hooper could be another Thomas Hooper, well Robert finally found that missing bank statement. It was hidden inside a set of his accounts for nineteen seventy four. I forgot to bring it but there's a payment dated November the tenth, nineteen eighty two, to the letting agents for the same amount as the deposit for the flat”. Gillian paused to hear Mary's reaction.

“I can't argue with that then”. Mary sighed. “I did know really. I just didn't want to believe it. He wouldn't have used a false name if he'd been a different Thomas, and he was away from home for two or three months at a time. And when he was home he had no interest in me or Thomas and Daniel. You can understand now how I relied on Tony, your dad”. Mary added, satisfied that she had now justified her relationship with Tony.

“How is Robert anyway ? I suppose Jane and Gianni have gone back home”. “Oh, Robert's okay now he's all sorted out. Jane went home last Monday, they've asked us over to Rome for a holiday". Gillian said excitedly as she handed Tony and Mary a hot mug of tea. Tony carried his mug back into the kitchen and began opening cupboard doors. "There's a fresh loaf in the tin and plenty stuff in the fridge". Gillian shouted.

"Holiday in Rome...that sounds nice, are you going ?" Mary gushed. "We've already booked our flight, we're going in the Easter break". "Will you be alright ? How're those ribs now ? And my lovely grandchild ?" "I'm feeling fine mum, I'm still six months away, Debra's baby will be your first".

"Tony returned carrying two plates of sandwiches. "There's a pile of mail on the hall table". He stated. "So you and Robert are off to Italy" He added and quietly whispered. "We'll pay your flight for an Easter present". "What's he offered you ?" Mary asked, not quite managing to hear every word. "Dad said you'd pay for our flight". "Just as long as you remember, we expect to be put in the very best home when we've gone doolally". Mary joked.

"I'm going to get off home now mum. Dad's seen the food in the fridge, but don't forget to look in the oven. I've made you a cottage pie. It needs cooking". Gillian informed as she walked towards the front door. "This pile of post will pass the evening, if you've got nothing better to do". She added. "Cheeky devil".. Tony replied with a sheepish laugh. "Bye then Gillian, we'll call round in the week and bore you with our photos". Tony said as he followed Gillian to her car and with a further trip retrieved the luggage from the Mercedes.

"Susan rang this morning". "How's your mum ?" Tony asked. "She's had a bad cold and it's knocked her about, Susan doesn't think she'll last much longer. The doctor was afraid it might turn into something worse". "She is ninety six, it's a big age". Tony remarked sympathetically. "By the way, Susan laughed her head off when I told her about your stupid Rossano Brazzi impersonation. She asked, how did you know ?" "Never you mind....I knew". Chirped Tony. "It wasn't him who actually sang in the film, it was some opera singer". Tony added. "Susan was surprised that you didn't let on that you knew what she'd said when she saw your photo". "Well I took a look in the mirror and decided she had a point". "Bighead". Mary quipped with a loud laugh.

"We're still going over to my house this afternoon ? We've still got to decide what to do with it". "Personally I think you should hang on to it, you don't need the cash, you'd be better off letting it for a couple of years". Mary replied. "I'll see, I want to have a word with the estate agents first, there's no rush". "Lets get going, you've probably got a pile of mail of your own to sort out. I'll go through mine when we get back". Mary muttered, placing her hand on the two inch high pile of unopened letters and assorted junk on the way to the front door.

"Can we go in my car ? I wouldn't mind giving it a run". Mary suggested, handing Tony the garage key. "Your car started no bother". Tony said after reversing the silver Mercedes from the garage. Mary climbed into the driver's seat and waited while Tony closed the garage door.

It took a thirty minute drive before Mary drew the car to a halt within a few feet of Tony's front door and waited as Tony quickly wandered around the outside of the substantial looking property. "Except for a couple of wheelie bins blown over, it all looks okay". Tony called out as Mary locked her car doors and stared at the house before following into the large entrance hall. “It's nice and warm in here”. Mary said, watching Tony shuffling the letters and loose papers together with his feet before making the strenuous effort to bend and pick up all the material that had been delivered over the past three weeks.

“Yes, I'm glad I left the heating on low, it's a bit of a damp old building otherwise. I'll find a carrier bag for this lot, we can have an exciting night reading our mail”. Tony said with a mischievous chuckle. “Well lets have a quick look round and go”. Tony added.

“I bet your postman wished he'd got a van”. Mary joked as she arrived at the end of the two hundred yards long private driveway and turned on to the empty country lane for the return journey.

“He has, we used to have a post box this end years ago, but it kept getting vandalised so my father got rid of it”. Tony replied. “Your house looks as if it would let or sell quite easy for someone looking for total privacy. You're going to have to decide what to do with all your furniture”. “It can all go, I'll get some fella to take the lot”. Tony commented. “Are you sure there's nothing you want to keep ?” Mary asked. “What's the point, you haven't any room for any more furniture, and we don't need it anyway, and if I tried to let the place I couldn't let it furnished unless I provided all new. Someone might give me a few quid for it”.

With the Mercedes safely back inside the garage, Mary and Tony sat in opposing armchairs each sorting through the letters and various items of junk that had landed on their respective hall mats.

After dispensing with all but half a dozen noteworthy items, Tony observed Mary holding a brown envelope in her right hand and gazing with a look of bewilderment at the letter in the other. “You look puzzled Mary, unexpected tax bill ?" "No....No.... Wish it was, here you have a read". Tony replaced his glasses as Mary handed him the two page official looking letter. "Wow.....that's a turn up". Tony frowned and dropped the letter on to his lap for a moment. "Foreign Office". Tony gasped as he proceeded to read in silence.

"They still don't confirm his death, they just refer back to the official investigation in nineteen eight three, and list him as 'missing person assume killed by persons unknown'. These documents they must have, they don't say how they got to be in the possession of this gang in Turkey". Tony paused and rose from his chair and knelt on the floor beside Mary, now appearing very distressed at the thought of her husband's fateful demise.

"It seems the trial of this gang started almost a year ago, according to this they had hundreds of passports and personal documents hidden when the Turkish authorities raided a building near Konya, wherever that is, never heard of it". Tony remarked..

"How could they have got hold of Thomas's documents ?" Mary asked still sniffing into her tissue. "I suppose whoever killed Thomas took his personal possessions and sold them on. That's all I can think". Tony replied and after a short pause, continued speaking. "Anyway it says now the trial is over they expect to receive Thomas's belongings very soon, and then they will be forwarded on to you".

By now Mary was visibly trembling with the thought of seeing and holding Thomas's belongings after twenty five years.

"According to the date on this letter it must have come a couple of days after we left". Tony uttered. "One thing for sure it's a bit of a jolt for your book when you get on to it". Tony added.

"Even now he's still haunting me, I knew I hadn't heard the last of him. It's bad enough with the complicated family situation he created. What with Thomas and Daniel now half brothers to Gillian and also to Robert and Jane, and yet Gillian is only related by marriage to Robert and Jane's her sister-in-law. And to back it up you're Gillian's dad. Good God what a strange family". Mary chuntered.

"It's all sorted itself out, I haven't heard Gillian say anything about Thomas and Daniel, she seems to have accepted it. I think the most important thing for Gillian and Robert was to find out they were legally married. And for me to have her know I'm her dad". Tony replied with satisfaction. "The only thing that really surprised me was that Jane couldn't be sure the photo of Thomas was her dad, she could only vaguely remember what he looked like". Tony added. "She was only six or seven and he was a bit hit and miss dad in between countries and here with me, she probably didn't see much of him". Mary replied.

"By the way, I have made a start, I've written seven chapters up to yet". Mary muttered. "You kept that quiet". "I didn't intend telling anyone until it was finished, but now we're living together there's no chance of keeping it a secret. I'll probably get fed up and ditch it anyway". "What next ?" Tony asked. "I suppose we ought to tell Gillian and the boys".

****

CHAPTER TWENTY

"You've been gone a long while". Mary stated as Tony was closing the front door. "It's freezing out there today. Yes, the agent was nearly an hour late, I was about to give up when he arrived. Apparently he had some family problem".

"Everything okay ?" Mary asked. "I think I'm going to sell the place, he went over all the aspects of letting, he said realistically to rent it out, it would need a total refurbishment, new kitchen and bathroom for a start. I can't be bothered doing that lot, I know the electrics and the plumbing's all okay, they were done a few years ago. And the lane will need resurfacing in a couple of years, there's a few potholes I hadn't noticed. So sod it, I'm going to sell it".

"Did he give you any idea what to expect for it ?" Mary enquired. "Not as much as I thought it would fetch, three nine fifty in it's present condition. I'll ring him tomorrow and tell him to put it on at four hundred and ten thousand. Anyway lets have some lunch and go dancing".

Several couples dancing to the first waltz were pulled up sharply as the keyboard player changed tunes mid dance and proceeded to play The Wedding March as Tony and Mary entered the room. A couple of holiday guests looked bemused as the regulars laughed and applauded.

"Glad to see you back, did you have a good cruise ?" Les asked while reverting to the original tempo. "It was lovely". Mary answered.

"Complimentary afternoon for you two....only today mind". Les chuckled. "Thank you very much". Mary replied. "You go first Mary, we'll have to run the gauntlet now to get to our table". Tony added. After twenty minutes of chat, back slapping and cheek kissing the newly weds reached their usual table and continued to enjoy the afternoon dancing.

The microphone made a high pitch screech when Les the keyboard player lifted it to speak. "Mary and Tony, will you please take the floor for the interval waltz ?" A slightly embarrassed Tony took Mary's hand as they obeyed Les's request to the gentle applause of the other guests. "I'll be your sweetheart if you will be mine........" Les sang softly accompanying himself as he played the melody.

After Tony and Mary had completed one circuit of the dance floor they were joined by a few other couples and as the dance ended it appeared that every one had joined in. "I presume that's some sort of compliment, no one sitting out". Tony quipped.

A surprise awaited the new married couple when they returned to their table. "We're certainly being pampered today". Mary gasped, seeing their table adorned with a pristine white cloth laid out with teas and cream cakes.

"I wish they hadn't done this". Tony muttered. "Stop fussing, we've been here every Tuesday for the past twenty five years, they all know us well. Just quickly stand up, say thank you and enjoy it". Mary said sharply. Tony duly obliged and again received and enthusiastic cheer.

"That was some afternoon, never expected that reception". Tony remarked as they left the hotel car park. "Yes, it certainly was, it's nice to know we're very well liked though". Mary responded.

"Just a thought, do you think Thomas's package might turn up soon ? It could come anytime, will it be small parcel ?". Mary wondered. "I've no idea, stop worrying, it'll be a while yet, it's only been three weeks, it could be another six months before it turns up". Tony replied.

"I need you to sign". The friendly postman requested as he handed Mary the sturdy looking jiffy bag. Mary felt her pulse racing in anticipation of the contents that the package would contain, and must have appeared a little abrupt and rude as she quickly closed the door leaving the postman standing out in the cold and wet on the mid April morning, without so much as a 'thank you'.

"The estate agents phoned, they've got someone viewing tomorrow morning". Tony shouted as Mary paused staring at the inside of the front door before slowly making her way into the kitchen. "You alright ?" He asked earnestly. Mary dropped into one of the four wooden upright chairs and glared at the unopened package laid on the kitchen table.

"Oh.....it's turned up then, are you going to open it ?" Tony could see Mary's hands rapidly tapping the pine table surface. "What are you so nervous about ?" Tony asked, now holding both her hands to prevent them from violently shaking.

"I just had a horrible thought that what's in this jiffy bag must have been handled by the person who murdered Thomas". Mary gasped out and immediately burst into uncontrollable tears. Tony pulled up a chair and sat down close to Mary and after a few minutes of consoling, the tears subsided and Mary regained her composure.

"Well, we've waited over a month, now it's here I suppose we'd better see what's inside". Mary urged, and sniffled a couple more times into her tissue. Tony cut through the stitched light brown, twelve by nine inch size package to access it's contents.

Mary gingerly lifted the sealed inner packet from

the bag and visibly shuddered at the sight of her husband's black leather wallet through the clear plastic wrapper. The last time she saw this, being the day she last saw Thomas when she waved him off on Plymouth station twenty five years ago.

Tony then lifted the wallet with his thumb and forefinger as if it was something unpleasant, causing some grains of sand or dust to fall out onto the kitchen table, together with a brief official covering letter describing the contents of the package.

“”I don't know whether I want to see inside”. Mary uttered with a slight tone of fear in her voice.

The short fastener strap was missing it's half of the press stud and the general condition of the wallet showed it's age.

“Here goes then”. Tony exclaimed as he slowly opened the wallet and placed it down on the table and removed the contents from one compartment.

“That's his work permit and this looks something medical and I don't know what this scribbled note is on this old envelope”.

At this point Mary produced a newspaper and stretched it out on the table. “Put it all on the paper, you've no idea where it's been or who's messed with it”. She instructed. Tony obeyed with a wry smile. “There's no passport....there's nothing in any of the other compartments”. Tony said with an air of disappointment as he again tried to read the writing on the back of the postcard size envelope.

“There's something inside”. Tony said, feeling the stiffness of the envelope. “I though it was just hard from being dried out. A photo, two photos”. He chirped with surprise as he carefully unstuck them separately and removed them from the envelope.

“They've got damp sometime”. Tony stated, and he laid the one water stained coloured photograph face up on the newspaper. “She's a good looking young woman”. Tony said. “Well she's not me”. Mary snapped in disgust as she stared at the coloured slightly stained picture of a dark haired attractive slim woman in her mid thirties.

“”Have a look at this one”. Tony said, emphasising every word as he attempted to hand Mary the other six by four inch black and white photograph, then promptly placing it on the newspaper. Mary gazed in astonishment. “It's the same woman, looks as if it was taken in hospital.

The two babies in her arms must be twins”. Tony said as he and Mary stared thoughtfully at each other. “Are you thinking what I'm thinking ?” Mary asked. “It looks like it was taken by a professional photographer, it's been stamped on the back, but it's impossible to read”. Tony added.

“If the lady is who I'm thinking of”. Mary said abruptly. “You think she could be Robert and Jane's mother”. “You obviously think so as well”. Mary noted. “Who are the two kiddies ?” Tony asked, having already assumed their identities. “I'd say the one must be Jane and the other......must be her twin sister, they both look like girls. The one must have died. Oh my God this is going to be another shock for Robert. I'll ring Gillian as soon as she's home from school, Robert will want to see these photos”.

“I'll put everything back in the bag it came in for now and we'll have some lunch”. Tony decided. “Before you do anything, wipe the table with the Dettol”. Mary insisted. “I really thought I had the perfect ending for my book, now this”.

“I'd say that's Gillian's car just stopped on the drive”. Tony remarked as the car headlights illuminated the hallway. “I'll go”. The whole of the

garden was now lit up by the security lighting as .
Gillian and Robert approached Tony standing with the front door firmly held open against the strong offshore wind.

"Sorry it's so late, but Robert just couldn't wait until tomorrow. It's his fault we're this late, he only came home half an hour ago and we came straight out". Gillian blurted out. "That's alright, we hadn't been in bed long". Tony joked.

"How are you feeling now Gillian ?" Mary asked. "I'm fine now mum, I've been discharged from the hospital now, just need to see my own doctor next week". "That's good but you really shouldn't have gone back to work yet". Mary replied.

"I was going up the wall with nothing to do. The school made sure I only do light duties, they've given me a classroom assistant to help with my little ones". "Well as long as you know what you're doing". Mary added. "I told Robert we shouldn't have come round this late, but he couldn't wait". "That's alright, it's obvious he'd want to see the photos. Can I make you a sandwich Robert ?"

Mary again opened up a newspaper and spread it over the kitchen table before Tony dropped the jiffy bag in front of Gillian and Robert.

"The photos are in that envelope, they're a bit grubby, they were stuck to the envelope, they must have got damp". Tony informed as Robert took the contents from the wallet.

Robert paused and stared at the photographs, holding one in each hand. A river of tears ran down and dripped from his chin and fell like raindrops onto the newspaper. Gillian watched in silence as he quickly wiped away the water from his face.

"I don't know what to think". Robert sighed. "I assume if this is my mum on both photos, and one of the babies must be Jane, but who is the other.

They're both girls aren't they ? Do you think she died ?" "That's what we thought must have happened. Unless the other child belongs to another mother in the hospital and she's just being photographed holding the two of them". Mary suggested. "No I think they are twins". Gillian chipped in, stressing the word 'are'.

"Jane should surely recognise her if it is our mother". Robert stated. "I would think so, but she wasn't very sure about Thomas when she saw his photo". Mary uttered.

"We're going to stay with them in a couple of weeks time, can we take the photos ?". Gillian asked. "Of course you can, Tony can print us some copies.....Here's your sandwich Robert. Wash your hands after handling that wallet". Mary instructed forcefully. "How about you Gillian ?" "Just a cup of tea for me mum".

"Robert, it's twenty past eleven, we'd better get going". Robert picked up the photographs for another look before putting on his anorak to face the cold night air.

"Tony will take some prints tomorrow when he pops to his house". Mary said as she and Tony followed Gillian and Robert and waited in the open doorway until the red Fiesta reversed onto the road and sped away.

"I imagine he'll ring Jane, he reckons he's not going to tell her about the photos, he's only going to tell her he's got a surprise. He wants to be there when she sees them". Mary said. "Some surprise that'll be". Tony quipped. "Anyway, do you want another drink ?" Tony asked. "No thanks, I'm going straight to bed, you can lock up".

****

CHAPTER TWENTY ONE

“That was the estate agent, we've had an offer on the house, not very good. Three hundred and sixty thousand”. Tony grunted. “You're not thinking of taking that ?” Mary asked crossly. “No, they taking the Mick, fifty thousand below the asking price....... They're trying it on. I told the agent not less than four hundred thousand, he's going to ring me back”.

“What time are you leaving to watch the lads game this afternoon ?” “Tom managed to squeeze me in on the team bus, he's picking me and Robert up at twelve and dropping Elaine off, so you can have a girly natter all afternoon”.

“Robert should be here soon”. Mary added. “This Counties cup final worked out just right for Robert, they're flying to Italy tomorrow morning, he'll only miss the last match of the season”. Tony replied. “I'll make us an early lunch, unless you'd prefer to take a sandwich with you ?” Mary suggested. “A sandwich is fine but I'll eat it here with a cup of tea”.

With the three menfolk all en route to Truro for the afternoon and most of the evening, Mary and Elaine settled in an armchair each in front of the log glow effect electric fire.

“You haven't seen these photos yet”. Mary said, handing the two postcard size prints to Elaine. “They're copies, Robert's got the originals to show to Jane”. “Tom told me all about his dad's wallet turning up.... his dad......it's Robert's dad as well...... and Daniels, What a strange situation. Jane's not seen them yet ?” “Not yet, Robert wants to show them to her, I can't wait for Gillian to ring and let me know what Jane says, and if it is their mother”.

Mary gushed excitedly. “And what about the other baby in the photo, I wonder what she'll think about it possibly being her twin sister”. Elaine murmured.

“Do you think Jane will recognise the woman if she is their mother ?” Elaine asked after a short pause. “”I would think so, I can remember what my mother looked like when I was a child. Mind you she wasn't sure about Thomas being her dad when she saw a photo of him. We'll know by tomorrow night, all being well”. Mary replied.

“Take the seal of this film while I make a cup of tea. It's an old film, I hope you haven't seen it”. Mary said. A few minutes later Elaine entered the kitchen swearing at the stubborn box. “Have you got a sharp pointed knife there Mary, the plastic seal's impossible to get off, it's so strong”. “Try the bread knife”. Mary suggested.

Both women returned to the the lounge. Mary loaded the film disc into the machine player and they both settled into the comfort of their respective armchairs. “One hundred and two minutes”. Mary said, reading out the details on the disc case. “That should take us nicely up to dinner time”. Mary added while aiming the controller at the DVD player sat on the shelf beneath the television.

“How long have you three been here ?” Mary asked, suddenly being disturbed from her nap in the armchair by their combined laughter. “We've just this second walked in”. Thomas answered as he gently tapped his wife on the shoulder. “Wake up dreamer”. “I wasn't asleep, was I ?” Elaine asked embarrassingly. “At least you both had your mouths shut, makes a change”. Tony joked. “He'll pay for that later”. Mary informed Elaine with a laugh.

“We've left your dinners in the kitchen, give them a few minutes in the microwave, not that you deserve any after that comment". Mary said jokingly.

"I assume you lost, seeing you're keeping quiet about the match". Elaine called out to the men sat at the kitchen table. "Don't ask". Thomas shouted back. "We were up against the winners of the Counties first division. We play in two leagues below them so we did well to reach the final". Robert said proudly.

"You still haven't said the score". Elaine ribbed. "Six one". "Your team got one kick of the ball then". She added, raising a loud laugh from Mary. "We'll stop it now, we're being horrible, enjoy your dinners". Mary said.

"I'm going to have to shoot off, Gillian and Maxine will be back from the cinema by now, and we've still got some packing to finish". Robert said.

"You're flying from Bristol". Tony confirmed. "Yes, we thought that'd be easier than going to Gatwick, mind you we had to accept an early flight. We've got to leave about five in the morning". Robert answered.

"We'll be going as well mum. Blimey, my legs are stiff, I think our last match next weekend will be my last. I'll just watch the lads next season, unless I'm offered a non playing job". Thomas muttered as he hobbled along the hallway.

"Right, now it's just you and me Tony, lets have half an hours tele, what's worth watching ?" Mary asked as she stretched full length on the settee and Tony settled back into his favourite armchair.

"That's the car cleaned for another month". Tony said having returned from a visit to the hand wash. "I thought you said you'd never go there again after the last time. Is it any better ?" Mary grunted sarcastically. "It is, probably because I had a moan about it they gave it a free valet service. If it wasn't so cold I'd clean it myself". "No you wouldn't....you've never ever cleaned your car, you've always gone to the car wash, you know you have". Tony conceded the argument and vanished upstairs to the bathroom. "Typical bloke". Mary uttered to herself.

"How do you fancy a ride along the coast and a pub lunch ?" Tony shouted from the landing. "Not really, I'd sooner wait in, in case Gillian rings". "I doubt if they're there yet, she's not going to be phoning until tonight or more likely tomorrow". Tony replied. "Oh okay then I'll go and get ready, I'd like to get back about three just in case". "You've got your mobile with you anyway". Tony chirped.

"You were called yesterday at nine twenty two am, the caller withheld their number". Was the response to Mary's 1471 request. "No one's called while we've been out". Mary advised Tony as he closed the front door. "Give them time to get there, I told you, if she rings it'll be this evening".

"She's not going to ring this late, I'm going to bed, she'll ring tomorrow now". "You can go, but I'm going to stay up a bit longer". Mary replied indicating her disappointed. "What's the point in that ? there's a phone in the bedroom anyway". Tony scoffed.

Mary drew back the curtains and stared at the rivers of rain water running down the glass panes. "It's tipping down". Mary observed. "It's been raining all night, didn't you hear it hitting the windows ? You must have slept sound". Tony replied.

"This must be Gillian". Mary squealed, grasping the handset at it's first ring. "Hello Gillian that you ?" "Me mum, sorry I didn't ring yesterday, we didn't get to Rome until very late. We didn't take off until four in the afternoon because of the fog and then we got stuck in Rome airport for ages, some strike or something. Jane and Gianni met us and took us straight out to a smart restaurant for dinner. We went to phone but we only had Robert's and it was out of battery. Was it foggy at home yesterday ?"

"A little bit, but it soon went. Never mind all that, what did Jane say ?" "What was that mum ?" "It's only me telling your dad to listen in on the hall phone".

"It was her mum, she recognised her straight away. Seeing her mum made her very upset, but when Robert showed her the black and white photo of her mum and the babies she couldn't believe it. She couldn't stop crying. She got very angry wondering why her mum had never told her that she had a twin sister". "It is possible it was some other mother's child she was nursing". Mary suggested.

"She's so angry at the moment, she's convinced herself that the other baby is her twin, she didn't know who was who on the photo. She couldn't tell which baby was her". "What does she intend to do ?" Mary asked. "Well one thing for sure, she's determined to find out where she is, that's if she's still alive".

"We're trying to make out the stamp on the back of the baby photo, it looks as if there's a date ending with a six, we assume it could be nineteen seventy six, that's the year Jane was born. Gianni thought it must be the photographer's studio stamp. Jane's going to buy a magnifying glass when we go out. Did you know there's something written on the envelope ?" Gillian asked. "We noticed that but we couldn't read it". Mary replied. "We can make out a bit of a word. We think it says Victoria, that's the name of a place that was in Rhodesia, it could be something to do with the hospital". Gillian added.

"Gianni's working, so Jane's taking us around Rome as soon as the rain eases off" "You're not the only ones with rain, it's tipping it down here. Is Robert okay ?" Mary asked. "He's fine, he's put our wedding disc onto Jane's computer, he's boring her with the photos at the moment". Gillian quipped.

"He'll have no battery left again, I'll let you go now Gillian, let me know if you have any more news. Bye then". "Bye Gillian". Tony shouted.

"I don't suppose you thought to take a copy of the stamp on the back face of the baby photo ?" Mary asked Tony. "No, I never thought about it, we couldn't make it out anyway. Even if it is the photographer's name, we're talking over twenty five years ago, I doubt if they still exist".

"The rain's stopped now Mary, I'll nip along to Deb's for the paper while you get the breakfast, is there anything you need ?" Tony asked as he struggled with his overcoat. "Here....let me help, you awkward devil". Mary laughed as she released his left arm from an inside pocket. "You can bring a milk".

A sodden Tony burst in through the front door with water dripping on to the ceramic tiled hall floor, and with a quick look in the mirror at his bedraggled hair, took the stairs two at a time and into the bathroom.

"The heavens opened up just as I came off the sea front". Tony said, now almost dried out and sat at the kitchen table eating his usual cooked egg and bacon breakfast. "I thought you were being a bit ambitious, you should have taken your car. At least you kept the paper dry". Mary joked and began to snigger as the water continued to drip from his wet hair onto his plate.

"How was Debra ?" "She says she's fine. Daniel was in the shop as well. He's packed in his part time winter job for this year to help Debra and look after the shop after the baby's born". Tony answered.

"I think it's going to be a day by the fire today". Tony added. "It would be if you'd remembered the milk". Mary grunted sarcastically. "I want to see Debra, so I'll have a walk when this rain stops, and if it doesn't stop you can go again".

"Hello mum, the weather's better this morning, it's a bit chilly but at least it's dry". "Hello Gillian, any news ?" Mary replied. "It's Gillian". Mary shouted in the direction of the kitchen to Tony.

"We can make out part of the photographer's name and the town......looks like Fort Victoria. That's the name we thought was scribbled on the envelope. Fort Victoria used to be in Rhodesia". "You bought a magnifying glass then ?" Mary assumed. "No we never went out yesterday, Gianni brought one home from his office. Anyway, Fort Victoria doesn't exist any more, it's now called Masvingo. Jane is desperate to find the photographer, I suppose they could still exist in the new town".

"It's a pity that wallet ever turned up, it's causing nothing but trouble and upset". Mary interrupted. "I don't think Jane will give up, she's determined to find out about the other baby, she was up half the night on the internet looking for addresses. The only thing she found was an address for the Masvingo Zimbabwe Directory, so she's already written a letter to see if they have any records or information of any professional photographers or the hospitals when it was Fort Victoria and the names of any photographers there now".

"I do hope she finds her sister.......and of course she'll be Robert and Thomas and Daniels sister as well. What you going to do today ?" Mary asked changing the subject. "We're going to do what we intended to do yesterday, see the sights. I can't see Jane getting a reply before we come home, if she ever does, but I'll ring you again later in the week. Bye for now".

"I don't think Jane has much chance of getting any answers, no ones going to be bothered about looking for information after twenty six years. Especially with it changing to Zimbabwe. The only good thing is that Jane and Robert have a photo of their mother". Tony chuntered having listened to the conversation on the hall extension.

****

CHAPTER TWENTY TWO

"It's Gillian and Robert". Mary shouted to Tony as she closed the front door. "Where's your car ?" "We've dropped it off at the garage in town, it's only for a service. We had a nice walk back along the prom, didn't we Robert ? That's something we don't do very often". "What time did you get back from Rome". Tony asked. "We landed at nine o'clock but by the time we collected the car and drove home it was well after midnight".

"Did you enjoy your break with Jane and her husband ?" Mary asked. "It was lovely, once Jane decided not to do anything else until she got a reply to her letter. It was cold though, about the same as here. I threw some coins in the fountain, we'll show you the photos next time. Jane gave Robert a beautiful photo of their mum, she had it cleaned and enlarged and put into a lovely gold frame as a present". Gillian replied.

"I imagine you want to find out what happened to the baby as well Robert, she's your sister after all". Mary asked. "Yes, course I do, Jane's going to keep me up to date. We're just hoping something comes from Jane's letter to this Directory for Business people. I'm just glad to know what my mum looked like". Robert said with a heavy sigh.

"Do you have a time to collect your car ?" Tony asked. "They said about a couple of hours, but they would give me a call". Robert answered. "You might as well stay and have some lunch, Tony will run you to the garage when it's ready". Mary added.

Susan rang this morning while you were at Tesco's, she wanted to know how Gillian and Robert got on. I said you'd ring her back". Tony called out from the comfort of his armchair in the lounge as

Mary entered the front door. “You could have told her”. “I thought you'd sooner have your weekly chat”. Tony chirped. “Suppose so”. Mary dryly replied.

“I've made some lunch, I'll bring it in to the lounge as soon as you're ready”. Tony said. “Oh good, I'm ready now”. Mary replied, throwing her top coat across the banister rail. “Be with you in a minute, just going to wash my hands”.

“I don't think Jane's going to get a reply to her letter, it's been over a month now”. Mary pondered. “I never thought she would”. Tony replied dismissively. “I think the whole thing's a waste of time. The Zimbabwean authorities won't be bothered”. He added.

“Well we shall have to wait and see, anyway this time next week I'm going to be a grandmother, all being well”. Mary said excitedly. “It's a lovely day, let's have lunch and go for a stroll on the beach, it'll pass the afternoon, we can call in the shop and see Daniel and Debra”. Mary chuckled. “So that's why we're going a walk, to check up on Debs”.

With all the immediate family and a few friends gathered around the font, the vicar gently poured tepid water over the forehead of baby Juliet.

Debra selflessly and very carefully handed her new baby daughter to Mary, who proudly carried her first grandchild out of the chill of the church and into the warmth of the late June sunshine. The brilliance of the white silk Christening gown contrasted vividly against Mary's midnight blue two piece suit, bought especially for the occasion.

“I shall be a grandma again next month”. Mary chuckled out loud, with an affectionate gaze in .

Gillian's direction. After numerous poses for photographs the party of sixteen strolled the short distance to Gillian and Robert's cottage, with Mary still carrying baby Juliet. “I've waited fifteen years for this moment. Debra, you can have her back, but only if she starts crying”. Mary joked as Tony held open the tiny front door.

Susan filled every ones glass while Elaine carefully removed the large sheets of tissue to reveal the array of sandwiches and fresh salads.

“It's self service today and it's all got to be eaten, so make a start”. Gillian called out from the corner of the cramped little lounge. “Maxine's serving teas and coffee in the kitchen”. Gillian added.

“I think we'll have to put a bomb under your mum, look at her, she's not going to let go of Juliet”. Tony uttered to Daniel. “That's all right as long as she doesn't mind when I call her in the middle of the night”. Daniel said with a laugh.

“If you have a boy you should name him after your dad”. Susan shouted across the crowded room to Gillian. “Tony or Anthony ?” Gillian called back. “I was thinking more Italian like Rossano”.

Standing within reach, Tony folded a magazine and playfully whacked a startled Susan across the back of her head to a chorus of laughter Susan joined in the hilarity and gave Tony a fond affectionate hug.

“Whatever you decide”. Susan added in her distinctive Midlands accent. “Don't choose a popular, or one of these trendy names. I always remember at my infant school, the first time the teacher called out 'Sue Ellen', me and five other kids all put our hands up”.

“I've already got the names decided”. Gillian replied, now standing by Susan's side with a plate of sandwiches in one hand and a coffee cup in the other....."Stewart for a boy and Katherine if it's a girl". "They're nice sensible names, I can see where they came from". Susan said approvingly.

"I never knew you had a second name auntie Susan". "I'm surprised that I have, your grandmother always said she didn't see any need to have more than one name, but I was the first and she gave me her mother's name. Your mum was named after your granddad's mum. She was just Mary".

"Uncle Walter looks as if he's enjoying himself with Thomas and Daniel". "Talking football I suppose, as long as he can talk football he'll rattle all day and night. He's probably half way through the history of Aston Villa by now". Susan replied.

****

CHAPTER TWENTY THREE

"Where's mum and Katherine ?" Gillian asked Tony as soon as he opened the front door. "Don't panic, she's wrapped her up well and just taken her for a little walk with the pushchair. She won't be long, she's only gone to fetch a paper". Tony answered.

"Was she alright through the night with you ? Did you and mum manage to get any sleep ?" "She woke up once for a feed, otherwise she was as good as gold". "I wish she'd do that for me, you must have some sort of charm over her". Gillian replied.

"How did your school reunion party go last night ?" Tony enquired. "It was okay, not many of my year turned up, but we had a good night. We got home about half one. Robert was a bit rough this morning but he struggled off to work. He finishes at twelve and he's coming round here to show you all the news that Jane's been sending him. I'm picking him up soon. Mum's not back yet so is it alright if I shoot off and leave Katherine for a bit longer ?"

"Katherine went off to sleep in her pushchair so I've not disturbed her, she's in the lounge". Mary told Gillian at the same time "shushing" Tony and Robert before they had even spoken.

"Right then young Robert, what's been happening, what's the latest ? What's Jane managed to find ?" Tony whispered.

"You know I told you Jane had that reply from the Zimbabwe office, not a lot of use, but they did suggest that the photographer could have located to a neighbouring country". "That seems to suggest they probably got out when it became Zimbabwe, or they were kicked out". Mary said ruefully. "Jane finally found a photographic firm with a logo that looks similar to what we could make out of the stamp on the photo.

This firm are in Pretoria in South Africa, next door to Zimbabwe. Jane said she spent hours on the internet searching web sites for photographic studios. Anyway she contacted them the day before yesterday and they emailed her back saying they did have offices in Fort Victoria and they did have a contract with a hospital to provide a service to take and sell photographs of new born babies. They added that the only original partner in the business recalls at the time that one of the babies was abducted from the hospital, and the police requested copies of their recent photos".

"You obviously think it must have been the baby in the photo then, Jane's twin sister, and your sister ?". Tony interrupted. "I can't see any other explanation, I suppose the baby could have died. Jane's more determined than ever to find her, or find out what happened to her". Robert replied.

"It sounds as if it's beginning to seriously affect you as well Robert". "It is....The other thing the photographic people suggested was to search the archives for the Rhodesia Herald". "And has she had any luck ?" "Not yet, I don't think she's had chance yet. There's a lad at school, he's only thirteen but he's a wizard with the computer, I'm thinking of asking him to have a search"..

"I can't see you or Jane getting any rest until you've found out what happened to her". Mary added sympathetically.

"Gillian, I think little Katherine is getting a bit restless". Mary uttered. "Yes, come on Robert we ought to be on our way, Katherine needs a feed".

Tony lifted the carrycot and placed it across the rear seat of the Fiesta while Robert collapsed the transporter and stowed it into the boot.

"We'll give you a ring the minute we know any more". Robert shouted through the open car window as he and Gillian waved as the car slowly travelled towards the sea front.

"Not so many holiday makers around now". Mary observed as they strolled along the promenade with Tony proudly pushing Juliet in her buggy. Juliet, now several months old and capably of all sorts of mischievous antics.

"She's took her shoe off again". Mary grunted while picking up the tiny pink item and popping it in to the pushchair, only for Juliet to chuckle as she tossed it back out onto the pavement. "That's the third time I've picked it up, if you think I'm giving you another go you're mistaken young lady. My back can only take so much. Here's your mummy". Mary said as they arrived at the corner stores to be met by Debra in the open doorway.

"You look made for the job". Debra remarked, referring to Tony holding the buggy handles. "She's getting to be a cheeky madam. She keeps throwing out her shoes, as quick as I put them back on she takes them off again and slings them out, either her shoes or her bonnet". "That's all the fun of being grandparents, it's too late to grumble, you always wanted to be a grandma". Debra joked.

"Thanks for having her, it's allowed me to look after the shop while Daniel went to the cash and carry. He's back now, he's in the store room......... Daniel". Debra shouted into the empty shop. "Your mum's here". "Hiya you two". Daniel greeted. "You've enjoyed yourselves this morning with the little terror ?" Daniel asked with a quiet laugh. "She certainly knows how to get you going, little monkey". Mary replied wagging a finger at a giggling Juliet.

"Has Robert heard any more from Jane ?" Daniel.

enquired. “We're going over to see them tonight, Gillian phoned just before we came out this morning, she said Jane's emailed some interesting information.....I could tell she was excited but she wouldn't say, she said they'd show us tonight”. Mary answered. “That doesn't sound like our Gillian, she normally blabs everything out”. Tony chirped.

“Anyway, we'll leave this little treasure with you now”. Debra lifted Juliet from the buggy to say goodbye to Mary and Tony.

Robert set his computer down on the dining table, raised the lid and pressed the 'on' button. “What you got there then Robert ?” Tony asked as he placed a chair for Mary and himself either side of Robert.

“A lot more than I ever expected, and one hell of a surprise”. “Show mum and dad that picture first”. Gillian urged excitedly. “No, we'll save that, lets look at the other stuff Jane's sent through first”. Robert insisted. “You've got me wondering now”. Mary murmured. “Right”. Robert exclaimed as he put some information on the screen. “This is the first of a couple of newspaper reports from the Rhodesia Herald from nineteen seventy six”.

“That's the same photo of mum with the twins that we've got, this must be one the photographers' studio handed to the police. I'll make it easier to read the article”. Robert said, enlarging the page.

“This all confirms the photographer's email about a baby being abducted. To think it could just as easily have been Jane that was taken. It actually states twin sisters born to Katherine Stewart”. Tony gasped. “Read on”. Robert instructed. “This is about a trial”. Tony said turning to Mary. “Yes I'm reading it”. Mary replied sharply.

"It seems a young woman was arrested for snatching the child from the hospital, but the case collapsed because she died mysteriously in custody. It states that it is understood that she'd informed the authorities that she had been paid to steal a baby girl by some unknown person, and an American diplomat was suspected of being involved"..

"Someone must have got to her to stop her giving evidence". Robert retorted angrily. "And it says due to lack of any further witnesses or information, the case was closed". He added. "That all sounds too convenient for someone". Gillian quipped. "Where did Jane find all this ?" Mary asked. "This is all off the internet, Jane said they spent hours searching. But Gianni investigated with one of his legal team through his firms contacts and found out that the baby was smuggled out of the country and given to a couple and taken to America". "My God". Mary exclaimed. "Let's hope they gave her a good home".

"This is all word of mouth, mind you, Gianni said no one could confirm any of this information".

"Makes you wonder who was responsible for that woman's death in prison". Tony suggested. "It's obvious she was killed off to prevent any further investigation". Tony added.

"Now show mum and dad that photo". Gillian demanded. The image appeared on full screen. "Yes". Mary sighed. "Jane". "It's not Jane mum, it's the lady who gatecrashed one of our wedding photos". "It looks like Jane". Mary added. "Jane took it to a photographic specialist's studio in Rome. They enlarged it and got rid of the glare and enhanced the detail of her face". Robert interjected, stealing Gillian's thunder.

"No...it can't be, you're trying to say it's Jane's

twin sister". Mary chuntered. "Well it is, it must be. She's the exact double of Jane". Gillian insisted. "Is this what Jane thinks ?" Tony asked. "Yes she's convinced, she's angry that she's lost the last thirty years of knowing her twin, she feels she always knew there was something missing from her life". Gillian stated.

"That's probably imagination, I know they say there's a strong bond with twins, but if she never knew she existed....it's just upset her and made her feel that way, I suppose". Mary uttered. .

"If it was the woman at the wedding, why didn't she say something, or make herself known. She didn't hang around, nobody remembers even seeing her. If it is her she must have been there because she knew Robert was her brother, so I don't understand why she just vanished. Unless she reappears we'll never know". Tony concluded.

****

CHAPTER TWENTY FOUR

"It's Gillian". Tony called out to Mary holding his hand over the speaker. "Yes Gillian, you okay ?" "I'm fine dad. We've got some great news about the photo". Gillian blurted, bubbling over with excitement. "Pick the other phone up Mary, Gillian's got some news". Tony said to Mary as she emerged from the kitchen drying her hands on a tea towel.

"We just popped into our local this lunchtime for a drink and got talking with Graham the landlord. He was asking about how Robert found out about Jane, so Robert showed him her photo. Guess what....He said he'd seen her before, he said she stayed for one night about a year ago, then the next day she suddenly had to dash off. He said she was the only guest that night and she spent most of the evening chatting with him at the bar. He said she was a beautiful lady, he couldn't be mistaken, and that he'd remember her anywhere. He said she was in the bar in the afternoon, on the Saturday, when she asked him if he would call her a taxi urgently. She told him something about her father being seriously ill and she'd got to get back home. She paid her bill and that was the last he saw of her".

"Didn't Robert say it couldn't have been Jane ?" Mary said jumping into the conversation. "Yes, he explained everything and showed Graham the photo of Jane's twin. He said it still looked like the same woman. He was amazed listening to Robert, he said he ought to write a novel about it". "That's my line". Mary interrupted again jokingly.

"He looked back in his guests register and said she'd booked for four nights. He told us not to tell anyone that he'd given us her name and address in America" "America ......That's fantastic news, well what's her name then ?" Tony asked.

"Her name is Louisa Johnson and she lives in a a suburb of New York, a place called Midtown in Manhattan". "Does Jane know all this ?" Tony asked again. "Not yet, we haven't had time. I phoned you the minute we got back from the pub, I'll ring you back later. Robert's going to ring her now". "She's in for the surprise of her life then, let us know what she says. Bye Gillian". Mary interrupted again and replaced the hall handset.

"Me again mum". "Blimey Gillian that was quick, has Robert spoken to Jane already ?" Mary asked. "He's just come off the phone. She's going to see if she can find the number for the address. Robert's going to have a look later on, he's had to dash off. He had a quick look on Google Earth but he couldn't decide which was the house. If it's the one he thinks, it's more like a mansion. Robert said Jane sounded shocked that she had actually stayed in our local pub on our wedding day and he could tell she was getting very excited".

"I can imagine she is getting very excited now with this information, I do hope it turns out okay".. Mary replied. "Robert's a bit annoyed, he had to go back to school for an afternoon sports period. I'm off for a couple of days with Katherine, so I'm just waiting now for Jane to ring".

"Thomas and Daniel keep asking if there's any news". "Yes, I know mum, Debra rang last night asking if we'd heard anything. It all seems strange, Jane is a sister to Thomas, Daniel and Robert and I'm a sister to Thomas and Daniel but not to Jane and obviously not to Robert, I hope not anyway".

"I doubt if you'll find another family as confusing as ours". Mary laughed. "And they'll all have another sister except me if they find this Louisa Johnson. I'll ring off now mum just in case Jane's trying to phone, I know she won't be yet awhile, just wishful thinking. Bye mum, bye dad, I know you're listening on the other phone". Gillian concluded.

"What did you make of that ?" Mary asked. "It all sounds very well but I still don't understand......we're talking about over a year ago, so why hasn't she attempted to get in touch since ? and the other thing puzzling me is how come she was at the wedding, Jane wasn't there and Robert didn't know any of this at the time, he didn't even know about Jane. I still think someone is going to be disappointed, I think it's pure chance she looks like Jane". Tony replied suspiciously.

"Don't be so ridiculous, we know Jane has a twin sister and she looks exactly like her, so who else could it possibly be ?" Mary snapped angrily. "I suppose you're right, it was probably Robert she had come to find. Still strange why she hasn't bothered to contact him though, I still feel it'll all be an anti-climax in the end". Tony replied apologetically.

"Well we'll have to wait and see, won't we ?" Mary concluded abruptly

"What do you intend doing with Thomas's wallet ?" Tony asked. "It's on the bench in the garage at the moment, I can't stand to have it in the house. I've offered it to Thomas and Daniel, Robert said he doesn't want it, so if neither of them want to keep it, it's going in the bin". Mary answered in disgust. .

"You're not so fussy with your car now the shines gone off it". Mary stated as Tony parked his Mercedes right next to the main hotel entrance doors. "I'm only thinking of you keeping your dance shoes dry". "That's new, we normally have to walk from the furthest corner of the car park in the pouring rain, just so you have a clear space all to yourself". Mary said sarcastically.

"What's everyone doing stood in the reception ?" Tony asked as they approached the entrance doors. "Sorry folks....no dancing today". Les called out as Tony and Mary joined the chattering group of disappointed regulars.

"Why is that ?" Tony asked sharply. "They've got a leaking roof right over the ballroom floor, there's buckets scattered around to catch the drips". Les the keyboard player answered.

"That's no problem, we're all old sods now, so it won't matter if a couple of us kick the bucket". One of the group shouted out causing a ripple of polite laughter.

More hopeful dancers arrived to hear Les repeat the reason for the cancellation as others began to depart. "We're here now". Tony muttered. "So lets stay and have a drink in the lounge, there's no leak in there, is there ?"

Tony and Mary followed by several couples made their way into the warmth of the lounge bar and settled for the afternoon into the comfort of the soft leather armchairs. "This'll do me for an hour". Tony said with his hands stretched out to feel the warmth from the log fire as a waiter entered the room

"Hey Mary, how's your son-in-law's search for the mysterious lady going ?" "He's still trying to find a contact number, his sister Jane over in Rome isn't . . having a lot of luck either". Mary replied to Pat, a close friend and her husband sitting opposite. "I think they're wasting their time". Tony chipped in.

"He's an old misery, doesn't believe anything unless smacks him in the face". Mary said jokingly. "You wait and see who's right in the end". Tony muttered.

An hour and a half later Tony and Mary rose from their chairs and with Pat and her husband Phillip were the last to leave. “See you next week”. “As long as it's not raining”. Tony replied, but his attempted joke fell on deaf ears.

Mary answered the front door, surprised to see Gillian standing on the step. Robert stretched across the rear seats of the Fiesta parked on the driveway and released the seat belt and lifted out the carry cot.

“We weren't expecting you two, I thought you had sports on Saturday mornings, Robert”. “We do, but the forecast was heavy rain for today, so it was cancelled, mind you there's no sign of rain yet”. Robert answered.

“Jane rang last night, we would have rung you but it got a bit late”. Gillian said. “Come on in, put Katherine on the settee”. Mary whispered as she fondly touched her sleeping granddaughter.

“It's a bit early to see you, something gone wrong ?” Tony asked, descending the stairs. “No, me and Robert are just going to Plymouth for the day, so we thought we'd call and tell you what Jane told us last night”. “I'll make a cup of tea”. Mary uttered.

“What's she found out then ?” Mary enquired anxiously. “She couldn't find a number for the address in Manhattan, but she searched the name Louisa Johnson. She said there was three in the area. The one sounding the most likely because of the age appears to be a very wealthy city company director. So Jane checked the company name and one of the other directors is named James Samuel Johnson. They were also listed as the joint owners of the company. She rang their offices in New York but the receptionist wouldn't give out any information about Louisa, and she said James Johnson was away on business for few days. She was asked to ring back in a weeks time”. Robert informed.

“Did she follow up on the other Louisas”. Tony asked suspiciously. “Jane said the other two names weren't right, one was too old and the other was a slightly different spelling. It was spelled Louise”. Robert added.

“We just thought we'd keep you up to date, just going to have to wait now till next week. Drink up Robert. Anything you'd like from Plymouth mum ? You can come with us if you want”. Gillian offered. “No thanks Gillian, but if you feel like it you can call here on your way back for dinner”. “Thanks mum but we've invited Maxine and her husband to us for this evening, you come to us, you know Maxine”. “No, no..you young ones have a good evening, we'll see you sometime in the week”. Mary replied.

***********************.

CHAPTER TWENTY FIVE

Tony was surprised to see Gillian's outline through the part glazed front door. "You again". Tony laughed as he opened the door. "We were only at your house last night". He added. "Jane rang early this morning, not good news". "Where's Robert ?" Mary shouted from the kitchen doorway. "He's had to go to football, he was a bit upset. Thomas called to our place for him, he's going to drop him back here after the match".

"What's happened then ?, come and sit down". Mary asked anxiously. "Jane rang the company number in New York again yesterday afternoon. The receptionist said Louisa wasn't available and eventually put her through to James Johnson".

"Well...what's the news that's not so good ?" Mary urged. "Jane said he was reluctant to speak to her until she completely explained the situation and told him she thought that she was his wife's twin sister. She had to ring off and email the photo of herself and of them as babies with their mother. He then rang Jane back straight away and told her the bad news".

"For goodness sake Gillian, what's so bad ?" Mary urged again. "Well Louisa was knocked over by a hit and run driver and has been in a clinic on a life support machine ever since. She's totally paralysed, but apparently she can see and hear". "Oh my God how terrible, the poor girl". Mary sighed. "How long has she been like this ? Have they caught the damn driver ?" Tony asked. "It happened at the end of July, a couple of days after our wedding, Jane never mentioned whether they got the driver". Gillian replied.

"So now we know why she's not been in contact. Did her husband say anything about her being at your wedding ?" Tony asked impatiently.

"He told Jane that his wife knew all about Robert but she hadn't been able to find anything about her sister. He said Robert was easy to find, and she hoped to recognise her twin sister at Robert's wedding. She said she got nervous and she didn't want to impose and spoil the wedding day. She'd decided to leave the introduction for later. But she had told him that she'd cheekily sneaked onto a photo so that when she did contact Robert he'd be able to see her". "That explains that, but why did she dash back home ?" Mary enquired.

"Her husband had to phone because her father had a massive heart attack, but he died before she got home. And then unfortunately three days later she was hit by this driver".

"How did she know about Robert, I assume she knew he was her brother ?" Mary asked.

"Apparently her father and his second wife had a nasty divorce, his first wife died when Louisa was a year old and he remarried twenty years later. Louisa found out from her step mother a couple of years ago how her father had had her abducted and she was not an adopted baby as she had always been told. That's what the divorce was all about, his second wife threatened to inform the police, but she never did". Gillian answered.

"How long were you and Robert on the phone ?" Mary gasped. "All afternoon, we had an extension each ?" "Why did Louisa dash home, surely she must have detested her father for what he did ?" Tony suggested. "No, apparently he'd been a fantastic dad to her, he'd looked after her on his own for most of her life, and it was only in the last two years she'd found out".

"She'd been told the name of her real mother and even the hospital she was taken from so it didn't take too much searching. She found out the address and then about Robert through tracing her real mother through an agency in America and finding out she'd died. The death certificate gave the address in Horsham. Her husband said they easily traced Robert but they never managed to find anything about Jane".

"So she assumed Robert and Jane would have grown up together and expected to see Jane at the wedding. Now she'll never meet them". Mary said sorrowfully.

"Yes she will" Gillian gushed with emotion. "Her husband is sending plane tickets for Jane and Robert and me and Gianni go to see her, he said that would make her dream come true. And they have three children for Jane and Robert to meet". Gillian said and immediately burst into tears.

"He was amazed how identical Jane and Louisa are when he saw the photo Jane had emailed him". Gillian continued, wiping her wet eyes. "I hope he's not expecting some sort of a miracle when she sees Jane and Robert". Tony said hesitantly.

"No, I asked Jane that, she said it was on his mind but he knows nothing can change her condition". Gillian replied.

"Where's Katherine ?" Robert asked immediately he stepped into the lounge. "It's alright I left her with Maxine for the afternoon, she's fine". Gillian answered.

"I assume Gillian's told you all about Louisa ?" Robert said sadly. "Yes it's a sorry story". Mary added. "I rang Daniel after the match, we'd love to meet her one day if it's possible". Thomas responded. "If you want to go, you can take my place, I'm sure Gianni would let Daniel have his flight, we'd have to have a word with Louisa's husband first". Gillian proposed. "No, definitely not, leave things as they are, we'll see her one day". "We'll take lots of photos with us". Gillian replied..

"One thing talking about photos, I forgot to mention was that Jane told Louisa's husband that if she hadn't sneaked onto that wedding photo we would never have found her, she said it was only because they looked so much alike that she thought it could possibly be her sister".

"Any idea when you'll be going ?" Tony asked. "I'm alright, school term starts again soon so Robert needs to check with his head. Jane's already said they can manage anytime. We just have to let Louisa's husband know". Gillian replied. "The only thing now". "I know...you'll need someone to look after Katherine". Mary interrupted.

Three weeks later the two couples travelled to New York to meet Louisa and stayed with her husband James at their luxury home where they also met their three children.

During their stay Mary received several email messages. 'No miracles mum' 'But Louisa definitely blinked an eye and a tear appeared when she saw Jane and Robert' 'All very emotional all round' 'See photos'. A very moving picture of Jane and Robert sat either side of Louisa's bed appeared when Mary opened the first attachment, followed by a happy family photograph of Louisa and James with their three children, two young boys and a slightly older girl looking the image of Jane at that age, and coincidentally named Katherine.

For almost a decade Mary led the perfect life. She had four more grandchildren, Gillian had another girl she named Mary, followed by a baby boy she called Stewart. Daniel and Debra had a second child, a baby boy they named Tony. Thomas and Elaine had resigned themselves to not having any children but two years ago at the age of forty three. Elaine had a baby boy and named him Thomas.

Except for the usual every day ills Mary and Tony enjoyed good health and tea danced each Tuesday afternoon. Mary finally completed her book, but with no sign of any opportunity to get it published the script remains as another file on the computer.

After the heartbreak and tears after meeting Louisa, Jane and Robert together with Thomas and Daniel made several trips to New York over the following years until Louisa finally gave up on life six years after their first visit.

.

oooooooo

Unfortunately Mary's idyllic life came crashing down three years later in early December when she became a widow for the second time.

****

.

CHAPTER TWENTY SIX

Mary sat motionless in her designated seat gazing at the almost deserted platform. With everyone now all aboard she felt a slight judder as the Eurostar began to leave St. Pancras railway station heading for the Kent coast. She looked sadly at the seat on the other side of the table, empty except for her coat and her day bag. Mary closed her eyes momentarily hoping that when she looked again Tony would appear sitting opposite her, she knew this couldn't happen but it gave her some degree of comfort to imagine him there.

Tony, Mary's second husband whom she married nine years ago on St. Valentine's day in two thousand and eight after a twenty five year romance, both then aged sixty six, died suddenly from a severe stroke just before Christmas. Mary made the courageous decision to proceed with the pre-booked rail holiday in memory of Tony, hoping it would relieve her loneliness. The train was now moving at speed through the open countryside as she glanced across the carriage compartment towards her fellow travellers wondering if she was going to regret her choice.

Mary hovered edgily amongst the rest of the party as they made their way to another platform and boarded the waiting train to leave Brussels and on to Cologne for the first over night stop.

Alighting from the coach transfer and entering the hotel Mary was relieved to see the large number of luggage items stacked in the reception area. After half an hour of informative talk by the tour manager, a rather stout man in his late forties, the guests gradually disappeared to their respective rooms.

Mary waited for everyone else to leave before collecting her wheel type suitcase, and with the excessively large plastic key fob held in one hand she dragged her luggage across the tiled floor to the empty lift with the other.

"I'll see to your case for you madam". Informed a smartly dressed young fair haired man as he followed her into the lift, appearing from nowhere. "Oh....that's very kind, but honestly I can manage". The young man ignored Mary's instruction and accompanied her to her door. "Thank you anyway". Mary said embarrassingly as she searched her hand bag and handed the young man she assumed to be a hotel porter a couple of euros.

Mary spent the spare hour before dinner exploring her room and carefully selecting her outfit for the evening. Her first thought was to dress down a little, not knowing what to expect from the other guests. "What the hell". She uttered to herself as she unpacked her favourite navy blue dress and smoothed out the odd crease. Now fully adorned in the very flattering slim fitting outfit with matching navy high heel shoes and clutch bag, Mary, still a slim elegant attractive lady took a final look in the mirror. "Not bad for a seventy five year old bird". She said again to herself. 'Must stop this habit I've got into of talking to myself'. She thought as she closed her room door and dropped the key fob into her bag.

Mary could see the dining room from the reception area as she left the lift, and that the thirty or so members of the party were already seated at two large circular tables. She hesitated at the open door and noted two empty chairs at the far side of the furthest table. Nervously she walked across the room trying to avoid any embarrassing stumble in . her high heels when a hand came from behind and took her arm and guided her to her seat and promptly sat at her side. The elderly couple in the adjacent seats immediately engaged Mary in conversation preventing her from acknowledging the companion who'd escorted her to her chair.

After a few minutes of interrogating Mary, the couple turned their attention to another elderly couple seated further along the curve of the table.

Mary noticed two euro coins on the table in front of her as she turned to speak to the stranger. “Ooh...you're the kind young man who carried my case”. Mary said in a slightly startled voice. “I'm ever so sorry, I mistook you for a hotel porter, how embarrassing” “I guessed you had, must be the suit, I always wear a suit”. “Well you look a very smart young man, are you travelling alone ?” “Yes, it looks as though we're the only two singles on this holiday”. “Aren't you a bit young for this type of tour ? except for a couple on the other table the rest of us are all past our sell by date”. Mary said smiling at the tall handsome young man.

The conversation ended for a while as the first course of the set meal was served. Having finished his soup in double quick time the young man picked up on Mary's previous comment. “I certainly wouldn't put you in the oldie category, just the opposite, you look very attractive, you look the youngest here”. “You're a cheeky devil, but thank you....flatterer”.

“I report on holiday resorts and tour operators for a couple of travel mags, this is only my first trip this year. So if you see me collecting literature and making notes you'll know what I'm doing. I do this for a break really, my desk job is as an editor, I check through manuscripts for would be authors”.

"How interesting, how did you get into this sort of work ?" Mary asked politely. "I suppose I was a bit brainy, I went to college then on to university, then I just automatically went into working in a publishers. I suppose my face fitted so that's how I got the job, all a bit boring at times, I prefer these tours, but I probably won't get another this year". "I'm sure you have your job on merit, how old are you ?" Mary enquired. "I'm twenty seven".

"I finished writing a story a couple of years ago, it's about two hundred pages". Mary said in a whisper so as not to be overheard by other guests.

The young man leaned closer to Mary. "Is it any good ?" He whispered back. Mary and her new companion began to laugh raising curious looks from the rest of the diners. "I think so, but no one seems interested, so it's still sitting in my laptop". Mary said.

"I don't know what to call you...I'm Mary". "Thomas or Tom...Horton". "My first husband was a Thomas, he was a foreign correspondent, he was killed in Asia a good many years ago. I've got a son Thomas as well, he's in his late forties now".

With the main course and the sweet now all served and eaten, Mary and young Thomas transferred to the lounge next door to be served with their coffee.

"So did you marry again ?" Thomas gingerly enquired, hoping he hadn't caused any offence "Yes......to Tony, but he died just before Christmas, we'd already booked and planned this holiday so I thought it might do me some good, I'm not sure if I've made the right decision". Mary replied sorrowfully.

On this note the conversation stalled for some time as Thomas could see that Mary appeared to get upset. "Anyway, If I give you my email address you can send me your script and I'll read it for you". Thomas said attempting to restore Mary's spirit.

Mary stood up from the lounge coffee table and thanked Thomas. “That would be marvellous, thank you, I'll send it as soon as I get home. I'm off to my room now, I'll see you at breakfast, good night and thank you for your company, I've had a lovely evening”.

The next morning Mary searched the dining room but there was no sign of her young friend. 'Is he avoiding me ?' Mary wondered, 'I am quite early' she thought to convince herself he hadn't deserted her as she selected a couple of rolls and a yoghurt from the breakfast bar and sat at an empty table.

The dining room chatter began to increase as the rest of the party together with another group of English speaking tourists gradually filled the room, with several of her tour companions wishing her a “good morning” as they passed her table.

Mary felt more lonely as each guest passed by, and with no one wishing to join her, she was about to return to her room. “Guten morgen young lady”. Mary looked surprised as the tall fair headed Thomas sat down beside her. “Young lady....for a young lad you've got some charm, I'm old enough to be your grandmother”. “You look just as young and attractive first thing this morning as you did last night”. Thomas replied with a sincere smile. “My God, I wish I was fifty years younger. I really do appreciate your company but you don't have to pander to an old woman”. “We're both on our own and I'm very happy to have a lovely friendly companion. I hope you're okay with me” “I'm delighted”. Mary enthused. “I suppose we ought to make a move, we're meant to be outside reception at nine o'clock. Have you left your case outside your room ?” Thomas asked.

Mary sat with the majority of her fellow passengers looking out from the first class Pullman carriage shortly to leave Cologne en route to Lucerne, watching as Thomas and a couple of the youngest members energetically loaded the luggage from the porter's trolley.

Thomas entered the carriage carrying his light grey suit jacket and occupied the seat directly opposite to Mary. The train smoothly drew away from the station and was very soon racing through the German countryside.

"Are you feeling alright ?" Thomas asked Mary. "You don't look too good, can I fetch you a glass of something ?" "No....I'll be fine, I just feel a bit queasy, it's probably only the motion of the train, it'll pass". "There'll be some refreshments coming round soon, you probably need some lunch". Thomas suggested. "Stop fussing Thomas, you remind me of my daughter".

Thomas leaned back in his seat and watched as Mary closed her eyes and immediately began to tremble and perspire. Thomas could see the distortion on Mary's face as a couple of age lines she'd cleverly disguised resurfaced.

Thomas and an elderly lady traveller sat in the adjacent seat instinctively approached Mary's chair and Thomas gently shook her arm. "Is she going to be okay ?" He asked the mature lady assuming she would know what to do. "She looks pretty poorly, shout for John". John the tour manager came immediately from his seat at the rear of the compartment, and was quickly joined by two other party members to see if they could assist.

"Mary...Mary wake up love". John urged. Mary slowly moved her head and opened her eyes and just stared vacantly at John. "Can you say something Mary ?" John asked, but Mary looked dazed and did not respond. "I think to be safe I'll arrange for an ambulance to meet the train at Lucerne"

The waiting ambulance standing in the station car park was visible from the train as it came to a rapid halt. Within moments two Swiss medical staff entered the train and were at Mary's side.

Thomas attempted to explain her symptoms as they proceeded a brief examination before carefully lifting Mary into a wheelchair.

"Does she have a relative or a companion travelling with her ?" The elder of the two medics asked in fluent English. "No she's travelling alone". John replied.

"You and Mary seem to have struck up a friendship, will you go along and I'll arrange to collect you from the hospital later ?" John asked Thomas.

Thomas collected his jacket and Mary's handbag and followed behind to the waiting ambulance.

The evening was getting late when John, the tour manager arrived at the hospital. "Sorry I'm late, how is she ?" John asked. "She's not too good, they've put her in an isolation room for the time being until they can find out what's wrong with her". Thomas replied as John followed him along the corridor to Mary's room."She looks out of it at the moment, we might as well go back to the hotel. They've kept a meal for you". John said quietly.

"I'll just have a chat with her nurse when she comes out". Thomas added. "You speak German then ?" John stated after listening to Thomas's discussion with the nurse.

"She didn't have a lot to say". John said having himself fully understood the conversation. "Well, lets hope when the doctor does see her it won't be too bad. We'll have to wait now for a call". Thomas concluded.

The warm morning sunshine greeted the group as they assembled outside the hotel before taking the short stroll to the lakeside terminus. "I'll catch you up sometime this afternoon. I'm going to pop over to see Mary". Thomas advised. "You know the itinerary, we'll see you later then". John answered as Thomas set off in the opposite direction to the puzzlement of the remaining party.

After a bit of confusion with the language dialect, Thomas was soon at Mary's bedside. Mary stared at Thomas in disbelief. "What on earth are you doing here ?" Mary asked in a strained barely audible voice. "To see you, how are you feeling ?" "Never mind me, you're wasting your holiday". "I'm fine, it's not supposed to be a holiday, I'm working and you're making it more interesting". Thomas joked, raising a forced smile from Mary.

Thomas could see that Mary wasn't any where near as well as she was trying to portray and that her concentration wandered and he realised she no longer acknowledge his presence in the room. "I'll leave you now Mary, but I'll phone. I might not see you again, we're off to Zermatt tomorrow". Thomas knew she hadn't listened to a word he'd said.

A nurse entered and ushered Thomas from the room. "The doctors think she has some form of fever, but they don't know yet what it is, but she's in the best place so don't worry. I understand you're just a friend of the lady". "Yes, but we're moving on tomorrow, so I don't know if I'll see her again. we only met on this trip two days ago"..

Every day for the rest of the eleven day alpine tour Thomas rang the hospital, but Mary's condition never seemed to improve and on the last night from the Paris hotel he was informed that Mary had been flown back to England.

****

CHAPTER TWENTY SEVEN

Mary returned to her Cornish seaside home to recover after receiving almost three months of intensive medical attention at a Hertfordshire hospital. Her health steadily improving and now being cared for at home by her daughter Gillian.

Gillian entered Mary's bedroom. “Oh good, you're awake mum. “There's a gentleman here asking to see you mum, name's Thomas”.

A vice like grip of fear immediately took control of Mary's chest as she drew a rapid intake of breath. Her mouth suddenly went dry and her pulse began beating like a drum.

Her mind flashed back to the last time she saw her husband leave from Plymouth railway station in 1983 and the vision of his black leather wallet laid on her kitchen table.

Gillian was completely oblivious to her mother's plight as she called down the stairs. “Come on up”. Mary became more panic stricken and gripped with anxiety with each footstep she heard as he climbed the stairs.

This was the moment she once dreamed of but now was dreading. 'I always knew he'd turn up one day, where had he been all these missing years ?'. She thought. Mary could hear Gillian whispering the other side of the bedroom door as it slowly opened.

“Guten morgen young lady”. Greeted the tall fair haired young man with a cheeky grin on his face. Mary's lungs instantly deflated and her panic attack drifted away with the relief of recognising the handsome stranger as he leaned across the bed and held both her hands and kissed her on the cheek, while at the same time leaving two euro coins in the palm of her right hand.

"Are you alright mum ? You look as if you've just seen a ghost". Gillian asked. "Yes, I'm fine now, just thought that......... never mind...everything's fine "Mary replied.

"What on earth are you doing here, it's absolutely wonderful to see you again Thomas, how did you find me ?" Mary gushed with astonishment.

"I couldn't have finished that holiday and never know what happened to you. I hope you didn't mind, I peeked in your handbag for your home address and phone number when you was in the Lucerne hospital. I rang your home and Gillian answered and she's kept me informed".

"Gillian, this is the young man I was telling you about". "Yes I know, Thomas rang me the day you were taken ill and we've been in contact ever since". "So you knew all along that he was coming here today, I wish you'd told me, I could have got dressed and put some make-up on. What a lovely surprise, I never dreamt of seeing you again".

Mary opened her hand....."They're the exact same two euros you handed to me when you thought I was the hotel porter in Cologne. You left them on the dining table". Thomas said. "I'll keep them safe as a memory of meeting you and the holiday I was never meant to have taken". Mary replied with a regretful sigh.

"I'm sorry but I'm going to have to dash off soon. Before I go I've got a present for you. Gillian sent me your manuscript. It's very good. I hope you don't mind, I took the liberty of having it edited and Gillian and I designed the cover and gave it a title"

Mary sat open mouthed with astonishment as Thomas revealed the smart looking paperback book that he had concealed between his newspaper. Mary gazed in amazement at the younger picture of herself on the cover staring across a Swiss lake,.

set against a mellow background, with the book title, 'Mary' boldly displayed above her head.

"That's beautiful, I assume you sent this photo of me to Thomas". "Yes mum, Thomas asked for some ideas for the cover so I emailed him that picture and a couple others". Gillian replied.

"It looks lovely but how did you manage to persuade anyone to publish it ?" Mary asked excitedly. "I never did tell you the real truth about my job. My family actually own the publishing company, and I was made a partner when I left university". Thomas answered. "But don't go thinking I did it as a favour. My dad's a pure businessman, he doesn't do favours for anyone. Your book really is a good story". Thomas insisted.

"I'll have to get going now Mary, take good care of yourself". Thomas said sadly as he hugged Mary and again kissed her cheek.

Gillian followed Thomas down the stairs and out to his car. "I doubt if I'll have any chance of seeing your mum again Gillian, but I'll definitely keep in touch. I hope her book does well, it'll be in the bookshops in a couple of months time. Bye then Gillian, lovely to have met you after all our conversations".

Gillian stood and watched Thomas's car disappear from view before returning to find Mary staring at the inside book cover with tears trickling down her face. Mary handed Gillian the open book. "You must have told him all this about your dad ? Read the wonderful inscription he's written especially the ending, that was his favourite song".

Gillian quietly read out the song title. "Till I waltz again with you", then slowly closed the book and placed it on the bedside cabinet besides Tony's framed photograph together with the two euro coins.

THE END

I am pleased and thank you for reading my story. I do hope you found it enjoyable and interesting.
I would be very grateful to receive your comments. You can review this book on line on Amazon Books.

Yours sincerely   t.a.wood

Printed in Great Britain
by Amazon